The Dark Wife

by Sarah Diemer

For Jenn--
always.

Acknowledgements

There are many more wonderful people than I have space to list who I appreciate immensely, and who supported me along the way—I am so grateful to every single person who helped me breathe life into this story and who believed in it. You know who you are. Thank you, thank you, thank you.

I am deeply grateful to the following amazing ladies for their insight, input, prowess and random awesomeness, without which, this novel would be a sad shell of what it ended up becoming. Bree, Jen, Maddie, Tara and my own Jenn were instrumental in helping me make my story beautiful. I could not have done any of this without you—I will never be able to articulate my gratitude deeply enough. Thank you.

Rhi believed in my story from the start (and wondered how it would smell), Rachel always knew I could do it (and, when I lost my way, reminded me tirelessly and wonderfully), Kat loved it (and it meant the world), Gemma was always incredibly supportive and wonderful, Jen knew this was "the one" before I did, Maddie has never stopped reminding me of who and what I am and Jenn read every draft and loved it as much as I did. Again, I cannot express my gratitude adequately enough—thank you.

My mom always believed I would get my books published. Always. When I was a tiny girl, she knew I was going to be a writer—that kind of faith moved mountains. Thanks for believing, mum.

My sister, Laura, is a paragon of intellectualism, bosom and talent, and without her staunch support, grandiose artistic abilities and constant belief in me and the story, it would not live. Thank you, kitty.

Jenn spun straw into gold. It is my supreme blessing that I married the most amazing editor in the world. She perfected this story—any errors left are mine. I love you, baby. Thank you for everything.

The Dark Wife

Before

I am not my mother's daughter.

I have forfeited my inheritance, my birthright. I do not possess the privilege of truth. The stories told by fires, the myth of my kidnap and my rape, are all that remain of me. Forever I will be known as the girl who was stolen away to be the wife of Hades, lord of all the dead. And none of it is true, or is so fragmented that the truth is nothing more than a shadow, malformed. The stories are wrong. I am not who they say I am.

I am Persephone, and my story must begin with the truth. Here it is, or as close as I can tell it.

~*~

"O, Demeter," they crooned, tossing flowers at her statue in the temples and sacred groves, anointing her beloved forehead with honey and milk, stretching at her marble feet in the throes of worshipful bliss.

In the Greece of long ago, gods rose and fell in prominence according to the whims of the people. Hestia was beloved, and then Hermes, and then Ares, and then the next god or goddess in a long history of mortal fickleness. One never remained at the peak of popularity for long, but my mother didn't worry. She was adored. To be fair, she loved the people as much as they loved her.

She loved me most of all.

"You will be queen of all the gods," she would whisper in my ear as we rested beneath her fragrant green bower. We listened to the hum of mortal prayers spoken through flowers blossoming upon the vines. She would simply clap her hands, and together we laughed as the wheat ripened and the grapes sprung forth along the long, low lines of arbor. Everything my mother touched turned golden, came to life, and I was in awe of her.

"You will be queen," she said, over and over, and I almost believed it, but I did not want it. Each time she spoke the words, my heart panged, and I changed the subject, showed her a hive of particularly fat bees, or the lining of a gull's nest, made perfect by its silver feathers. Her face closed up, and she made me say it, too, that I would be queen of all the gods, far surpassing my competitors in beauty and influence and charm. I was a new evolution, part of a generation of young gods and goddesses created not from foam or other mysterious means but through the power of their immortal mothers. Hera's daughter was Hebe, Aphrodite's daughter was Harmonia, and Demeter's daughter was Persephone. Persephone. Me. We repeated the litany while she combed and oiled my hair: it was in my stars that I would be greater than all of the others. And then, of course, Demeter would be greater, too.

I dreaded this with all of my heart.

I didn't want to be greater than the other goddesses—I mostly wanted to be left alone. I was a quiet child. I wandered the woods with my mother's nymphs. I could play with the pups of wolves or tigers, could climb the tallest trees, could eat any poisonous fruit I touched, and nothing would ever harm me. In this, in the beginning, I *was* my mother's daughter, and the earth cradled me as its own child.

I grew slowly, wild and tall, my reflection in the riverbanks that of a beautiful, sun-kissed creature. I was, after all, the offspring of Demeter, a goddess, perfection in flesh. I lived in the untamed green, lying for hours in sunbeams or cavorting with rabbits in meadows. These were my pastoral days, when I was free and not yet a woman. My life was simple and idyllic, though astonishingly empty, before.

Even now, sometimes, I dream of her.

Her name was Charis, and she was one of the nymphs in my mother's wood. For the most part, the nymphs were gentle creatures; they frequented the festivals of Pan, sought out other earthy creatures for pleasure. They were always happy in my mother's perfect gardens and among the trees, what was known, then, as the Immortals Forest.

Charis was not like them. She was a nymph, yes, but she carried the deep regret more common to mortals. She fascinated me, endlessly. "Why are you so sad?" I asked her, over and over, but Charis said nothing, wove flowers into my long, tangled mane. Her fingers were gentle, her eyes filled with tears.

She never spoke to anyone.

It was close to the anniversary of my birth. Most gods did not count their years—what would be the point in counting forever?—but my mother had jealously kept track of mine. Soon, it would be time for my introduction to Olympus, time for me to meet all of the gods, particularly the goddesses I had always been measured against. I had never been outside of the forest, my home, and the thought of leaving that beloved sanctuary woke within me a deep anxiety.

But I tried not to think about it. I made flower crowns, and the sun rose and set, marking off another day nearer the dreaded beginning of my future. Moments flitted by too fast, now that they were more precious, and it was three months away, my trip to Olympus, when everything changed.

The nymphs strummed their lyres at the edges of mirror pools, chatting on heroes and Olympus gossip. I sat at the edge of the water and their world, watching the clouds float over us all. Charis was beside me, and we shared no words; her presence was company enough. The day was new and warm—the days were always warm—and the air smelled of sprouts and ripe peaches.

Charis took me by the hand and led me to a tree.

I did not know what love was. I had heard the songs, had watched the nymphs grow besotted with satyrs and foolish mortals (foolish enough to tempt the gods' anger by venturing into the Immortals Forest), and I had witnessed heartbreak when lovers lost interest or, worse, were turned into trees or constellations because they had provoked the wrath of some god or other. If that was love, I wanted no part of it. It seemed so fickle, destructive, pointless.

That was before she kissed me, of course.

"I am afraid," I told her. We were sky-gazing together, seated in the arms of the broad oak. I was curled next to the trunk, and she was farther out along the lowest branch, close enough that I felt her warmth, smelled her green, mossy scent. My stomach was fluttering, though I didn't understand why—nerves, perhaps. Dread over the journey to Olympus. The days were blurring by, and I felt that I was about to lose all I had ever known.

"Afraid?" she asked me, uttering the first word I had heard her speak. My eyes grew wide as she leaned closer, shaking her head, the ever-present tears beneath her lashes unshed. "You should not fear, Demeter's daughter. You have nothing to be afraid of."

"Charis," I whispered. "Your voice…" It was the sound of rocks grating against one another, rough, deep, a bear's growl.

"I have been cursed for my past indiscretions," she smiled at me sadly. "I thought that, if you heard my voice, you would find a better companion."

We stared at one another for a long moment, feeling raging through me—pain that she had hidden her secret from me for so long, untrusting, assuming that I would, that I could, throw her away. I didn't know how to respond, but I forced out a whisper: "You're not a plaything to discard. I would never do that to you."

"Others have." And her tears began to fall. They streaked down her face, silver lines like the tails of comets. I touched her, just as we had done a hundred, a thousand times before: a finger to the cheek, a comfortable, comforting thing. She sat still, eyes closed, and permitted me to wipe away her tears, and when I was done, as simple and smooth as a prayer, she wrapped her arms about my waist, pulled me near her, so that she could kiss me.

I had seen nymphs do this amongst

themselves, and I had caught a hero and one of the tree girls trysting in the briar hedge. I knew what a kiss was, but not what it was for.

Now, there was softness against my lips. In my nose, her scent of wild green things, leaves and grass. And as she drew me closer, pressed me hard against her chest, I felt a fire catch within me. It was so hot, this new heartbeat that burned through my body, my skin, coursed down to my fingers and toes and back up again, and she tasted warm and good. I was drinking her in, and she kissed me deeper, and there was so much emotion in me, in every part of me, a pure, unbridled and impassioned joy.

This, then—this was love. I finally understood.

We met, that night, beneath the brilliant silver moon, Artemis's crescent hanging low in the eastern sky. We, too, found ourselves at the briar hedge, and there the moonlight patterned the lines and curves of her body.

"You are so beautiful," she said, moving her fingers over my skin until it prickled, then ached. She moved the linen away from my legs, my hips, as we lay down side-by-side and murmured together. In her arms, I felt things I had never felt, and she touched those places I had not yet understood. Perhaps I was naive, nearly a woman before I came to know all I could know about myself, about the solace to be found in another's embrace—but I don't regret it. That night, beneath the stars, beneath her, I knew love. It all came down to this: this moment, this touch, this kiss. It was easy and perfect, and I would never forget it in all of my immortality. I loved Charis in that hedge, under that moon, with all that I was.

"We'll leave," I told her later, when we lay twined together like grapevine. She nuzzled my cheek with her nose and kissed me softly, and I felt like I knew everything, that I could run away from my vile destiny and be happy: truly, forever happy. "We'll leave before my mother takes me to Olympus," I whispered, and she agreed, and that was that. The plan was made, and my heart sang. We would, both of us, be free.

Each day, we came together, beat new paths through the forest together, and each night I left my mother's bower to be with Charis beneath the stars. The days passed as we formed our plans. One month before Olympus, on the night of the full moon, we would leave in a little coracle of the nymphs' making. We would slip down the river and out of my mother's blessed garden, and we would find our way to the caverns in the northern mountains. Together, there, we would live and love.

In those lazy, golden afternoons, with Charis' black mane pillowed in my lap, listening to her heartbeat, winding my fingers with her own, the arrangement seemed flawless—perfect, like her skin and her scent and her laugh. I did not worry over the small detail that every place on this earth belonged to my mother, that there was, in reality, no place we could hide where Demeter would not find us and steal me back. I did not think about food—gods do not need to eat, but nymphs must—or shelter. Charis and I believed that the world would provide for us, as it always had, here in the Immortals Forest—here, where I was a goddess, and all creatures and green life must curtsy to me. I did not believe I would ever know anything less than that sweet privilege I had been born into.

The last morning was like any other. I rose and greeted the sun, sat impatiently while my mother combed out my curls and made me recite her favorite words: "I will be the greatest of all the gods, greater than Hebe and Harmonia. I will be the queen of Olympus." I muttered half-heartedly as she braided vines in my hair, spread my skin with nectar and flower oils. I sidestepped her embraces, pecked her cheek and walked out into the woods to find my beloved.

Everything was golden. It always was. The birds sang, and the animals lay, cooled by the springs and pools, as nymphs trilled songs of everlasting love and fed each other grapes from purpled fingers. "Have you seen Charis?" I asked them as I passed, and they said they had not, so I ran, deeper into the woods.

It was not like Charis to be absent from our favorite meeting place, the arms of that old oak where all of this, where we, had begun. But she was not there. She was not at the mirror pool. She was not further down the stream, and she was not in the willow grove, another of our favorite haunts. My heart thundered in my chest as I made ever-widening circles around the Immortals Forest, calling out her name. I stood in the center of a meadow, hands balled into fists, fear—for the first time—lodging itself deep in my belly, unfamiliar butterflies twisting and turning and beating against my bones. Charis was nowhere to be found.

I was trudging back to my mother's bower, heart pained, when I heard it. If I had not been on edge, my every breath an ache, I never would have heard so small, so soft a sound. I stood very still and listened harder—there it was again. A whimper. It was close, and though my heart skipped, I stood and listened until I heard it, placed it. There, there... It was there.

I had not yet looked for Charis amongst the briars, and the sound was coming from beyond the hedge. I slipped closer and peered through thorns and red flowers, expecting to spy a nymph and a satyr, expecting anything else, anything but what was there.

Charis lay on the ground, on our sacred ground, stomach pressed against the earth, mouth ensnared by vines that wrapped themselves about her body, twining and twisting, even as I watched. Behind her, over her, in her, was a man—a golden man who shimmered and flashed like lightning as he grunted and pushed. Over and over, he pushed. Tears fell and the vines tightened, cut into perfect ankles, wrists. My Charis was held captive as he did what he wanted with her.

Anger rose in me before I could think or make sense of what I was seeing, and I was shouting, shouting loud enough, I was sure, to be heard on Olympus, half a world away. I was moving through the hedge one moment, prepared to scratch and tear, when the man turned and looked at me, and I crumpled to my knees.

He was smiling, teeth dazzling white in a leering, dripping mouth, when he pulled out of her, stood, grew. He was taller than the tallest trees in my mother's forest, and then, with a great laugh, he fragmented, splintered into a thousand rays of light too bright—a thousand times brighter than the sun itself. I screamed, covered my face with my hands, and when I could see again, he was gone.

Charis, too.

I fell, dumbstruck. Where she had been, where that violent blasphemy had taken place, stood a small rosebush. The roses were white, dewy, and, as I watched, they moved in an unfelt wind.

I had heard tales of Zeus' conquests, He would zap down to earth, lustful, in need of something his wife, Hera, could not provide—or, perhaps she could, and she simply found him despicable. He had his way with whatever creature struck his fancy, and if they were not obliging, he punished them. Hundreds of times he had done this, perhaps thousands. I knew of these stories—the nymphs whispered them to one another—but, shamefully, they had never concerned me. They had never applied to me. But now, here—here was a nightmare come to life. The girl I loved had been raped before my eyes, and she was no more.

In that simple, ordinary space of time, I had lost everything.

I ran until the air burned in my lungs like fire, until I reached my mother's bower. "Persephone, what's happened?" she asked, holding out her arms to me so openly. My mother, my mother who could grow a forest from a seed, who could breathe a world to life. How I wished, hoped, that she could undo what had already been done. I wept and I told the story, and she listened, paling.

When I was done, she held me close, patted my shoulder stiffly. "Persephone...I'm so sorry. So...sorry. Zeus—he gets what he wants, and the poor creature cannot be changed back."

"She's gone?" I whispered. "But..."

All my life, I'd believed my mother could make the impossible possible. In my childhood imaginings, she could sing the moon down, change the pattern of the stars, unmake the world and build it new again, if she wanted.

Demeter removed her hand from my shoulder, moved away.

"There's nothing we can do." Resignation weighted her words. Her face was expressionless, hands shaking. "Please forget her. Forget Charis. It's what she would have wanted. You don't know Zeus—you don't know what he's capable of..."

There were tears in her eyes. I had never seen my mother cry. She reached for me, but I recoiled from her touch, stepping back once, twice. My mother was crying. It was unfamiliar, frightening. She seemed a stranger.

"Zeus did this," I spat, carving my fingernails into the palms of my hands. I felt anger grow and tighten within me, an invisible knot. "Zeus..."

Demeter opened and shut her mouth. Her face crumpled. "Zeus gets what he wants," she repeated, dully.

"How can you say that? What if that had been *me*?" I couldn't breathe, held my chest as if my heart was falling, falling, falling down upon the perfect emerald grass. "You wouldn't be standing there, you wouldn't say that, you would come get me, you would..."

She was staring at the ground, and the sudden realization devoured me. I stopped speaking, blinked at my mother.

"You would... You would come get me," I whispered. "Wouldn't you?" The words lingered between us for heartbeats, and then she shook her head, rubbed at her eyes with long, trembling fingers.

"He wouldn't do anything like that to one of his daughters," she said. "I don't think."

There was silence for a very long time. The loudest silence, and the sharpest. My mother kept her eyes on the wall of her bower, and I felt a thousand things shift between us. So many words unsaid, thorn-snagged, broken.

I was Zeus' daughter.

"You never told me," I whispered. "I thought you'd just created me—like one of your trees or your fields."

"I'm not that powerful." She worried at the edge of her garment, shifting it this way and that, staring down at the cloth and not me. "Persephone," she murmured. "I'm sorry… There's nothing we can do."

"Zeus is my father," I said, stringing the words together quickly, gulping in great lungfuls of air. "If he was raping me, you wouldn't come to my aid. My beloved is gone now, killed by Zeus, and you are going to do nothing to help me."

"That's wrong. Please…" She lifted a hand to touch me but dropped it when, again, I backed away. Tears trailed down her cheeks in bright, silent lines. "He can be so cruel, Persephone. You don't know. There's nothing I can do. Nothing anyone can do. I'm sorry. Please believe that I am sorry." And then, my mother, the goddess Demeter, held out her hands to me. Her voice cracked when she said, "Forgive me—I am glad it was her and not you."

What could I do? What could I say? She'd spoken her truth, and there was nothing left in either of us. All of the anger, the rage, the deep, abiding pain pooled from my body and drained into the earth. I was empty.

I turned, and I left my mother's bower. She tried to say something to me, but I didn't hear it, perhaps didn't listen, and I began to run when my feet felt the forest floor beneath them. I ran back—back to the briar hedge. I knelt down beside the rosebush, and I wept until my tears ran out. The rose leaves fluttered, though there was still no wind, and I felt everything I was break apart into tiny, tiny pieces. I had lost Charis, and I had lost our beautiful future.

My stomach churned as I dug my fingernails into the palms of my hands again and again, feeling the prick of them against my sore skin. I couldn't think about my mother, my mother with her tears and wide eyes and paled skin. But all I could see was her face, her mouth forming that most hated word: "Zeus."

I brushed a finger over the white petals of a rose, held it until I was white, too, hollow and formless, until I had become a beginning. Then, blank, I stood and turned, seeing, unseeing, the stars that had come out, the night sky that arched over me, blotting out the day.

In the sky swung the sickle moon and a myriad of constellations. My mother had told me once that the stars were uncountable, that Zeus had fashioned them endless—endless, like me.

Pain was slowly being replaced by something else in my heart, in my body, that I did not yet understand, and wouldn't—not for a while yet. That seed was growing, twining around my being, shifting the broken pieces into some new semblance of what it once was.

Zeus—my father—was king of all the gods, and he could do as he pleased.

And I would repay him, someday, for all he had done.

I, Persephone, swore it.

I left Charis where she was, roses and leaves waving beneath the grinning moon. Soon, soon I would be brought to Olympus, compared by the gods to my peers, driven from the only home I'd ever known to spend an evening in the same bright palace that housed Zeus. Zeus, the merry, golden god who raped and destroyed without regret.

What would I do when I saw him? What would I say? Would he punish me for the truths that might tumble from my mouth? My mother had looked so afraid.

I had to stop this.

I put my head in my hands, leaned against the old oak, tried to sooth the scattered aches within me.

Who does a goddess pray to? I sat very still, my head spinning in tight circles. We have nothing and no one to ask for help, save ourselves. I did not believe in myself enough.

The stars shone, silent as always. I folded and lay on the black earth, feeling the empty, lonely places in me crumble until nothing remained but blackness and the scent of white roses I could not see in the dark.

The Truth

One: Olympus

"Speak as little as necessary," she whispered in my ear, anxiety sharpening her words. "It'll be over before you know it."

I bit my lip but held my head high as Demeter pressed her hand against the small of my back, steering me toward the gigantic golden maw that would swallow us into Olympus. I breathed in and out and willed my hands to stop shaking. I did not look back at my mother.

One step, and then another, as we neared the opening to the realm of Zeus. No gods or demi-gods or nymphs or satyrs lingered around the gates—they were already inside, I imagined, drinking ambrosia and laughing uproariously at whatever crude party tricks they'd devised. This was the night I had been dreading my entire life. This was the night I would be introduced as a goddess to the Olympians.

My mother nudging me every step of the way, I moved onward.

Columns rose into the clouds, up and away from us. There was no ceiling within the Palace of Olympus, only unending sky that changed, at the gods' whims, to night, to day, to eclipse, to a hundred million stars. Distant lyre music teased my ears, and laughter, and as we crossed the palace threshold, a disembodied voice proclaimed so loudly, and to my horror, "The goddess Demeter, accompanied by her daughter, Persephone!"

Countless pairs of eyes—set like jewels in gleaming, perfect faces—stared at my mother and me.

I wanted to vanish, wanted to shrink smaller than a droplet, wanted to hide myself away in the deep, crumbling earth. In that moment, I would have given anything, made any bargain, to be gone from that place. My mother paused, waved to someone, and touched my shoulder gently. "Courage," she whispered, and I descended the luminous marble steps with my head held high, trying not to mind the whispers, trying to imagine that I was—once more— home, in the Immortals Forest. That I was with Charis, and the lightning bolt that tore us apart had never struck.

"Demeter, she is as lovely as you have told us. Lovelier."

The goddess who stepped near, laughing softly, dazzled my eyes. She was beautiful, more beautiful than seemed possible, or real. She wore the long white tunic of common Greek fashion, but it was woven of a gauzy stuff, diaphanous and revealing.

Pink roses twined her hair, and her smile was coy, infectious. I bowed my head in awe. Though I had never met her, I recognized Aphrodite.

"You are such a pretty creature," she breathed, embracing me fully, grazing a kiss against my cheek. She reeked of roses. "You have your mother's eyes."

Over her shoulder, I saw a girl, a girl like me. New to this place, this game. She was pretty, thin, eyes downcast, hair rife with pink blossoms, just like her mother's.

"Persephone," my mother said, though the introduction was unnecessary, "this is Aphrodite and her daughter, Harmonia."

I smiled, wondered if I should say something, started to, but Harmonia did not look up at me, did not step forward or offer her hand. She remained still as a statue while her effervescent mother laughed, brushing a white hand over her daughter's tight curls.

"Ah, I must find Ares, so I will leave you to indulge in the festivities. Enjoy yourself, Persephone. You'll never have another first time." Aphrodite winked at me, but there was a bitter turn to her smile. She cast her eyes about, grasping Harmonia's arm, and would have moved on had she not been stopped by a shimmering figure.

"Aphrodite, introduce me to your charming companion!" His voice was soft and sweet, but there was an undercurrent to it that I could not place. I looked up at him just in time to be kissed full on the mouth.

"Oh!" I stepped backward, raking my hand over my lips, but he was laughing, Aphrodite and my mother were laughing—Harmonia stayed dumb, still—and I felt shame steal over my face in the form of a maiden's blush.

"Persephone—meet your half brother, Hermes," said my mother, hiding her amusement behind a hand.

His hair was black and curled, and his sandals were winged. "Thou art as lovely as your mother informed us," he said, in mockery of Aphrodite, and bowed deeply, snatching at my hand to kiss it. "And I am the god of thieves and flattery and all that is wrong with the world. It is ever so divine to make your acquaintance!"

I had never met anyone who spoke so quickly. His words blurred together, as did he, flickering in and out of sight, a hazy outline trembling like a leaf in the wind, vibrating.

"I have another name," he whispered in my ear, then darted behind me. At the corner of my eye appeared a white rose, proffered to me by his shimmering hand. "It's Quicksilver," he laughed, and I brushed him away, stepped toward the long line of tables that groaned beneath platters of grapes and cakes, luscious fruits spilling out of golden goblets.

A white rose. Charis had become a white rose. Charis who was lost to me.

I leaned on the table and took a sip from one of the cups to steady my head. I had never drunk ambrosia before—it tasted of grapes and rare fruits, crushed and made perfect within the minds of the gods. It was bliss, but it wasn't real—they created it with their thoughts, their desires. I stared down into the swirling cup and realized I would be thought rude by Aphrodite, by the statue Harmonia. I had not excused myself. I had been thoughtless. I had behaved as if none of this mattered to me—and it didn't.

Still, I looked up and tried to find them, but they had disappeared in the sea of assembled immortals.

I sighed and lifted the cup to my lips again but froze in place before the drink touched my tongue. There, that man—from behind, and only for a heartbeat, I'd mistaken him for Zeus. Hot blood thundered through me. It wasn't him; perhaps it was Ares or Poseidon. But, still, Zeus was here. This was his palace, and he was ruler of all he surveyed. All of us. Somewhere in this great hall, he breathed, spoke, laughed, watched.

"I apologize if I offended." Hermes appeared so suddenly that I jumped, spilled ambrosia down the front of my dress. He waved his hand over the fabric, and the liquid beaded out of it, crawling over my breasts and down my arm to settle into the goblet once more.

I stared at him, and he bowed again. "I do not mean to startle."

I didn't know what to say, so I said nothing. He held out his hand to me, but I refused it, clutching my goblet tightly. Hermes shook his head, frowned.

"I heard what happened to Charis." Again, he whispered in my ear, lips so close they brushed against my skin there.

I stiffened. He had spoken her name, my beloved's name. No one had spoken it aloud to me since it had happened, and I murmured it myself only in the dark of night. I liked to whisper her name into the moving waters of the stream; the ripples caught and carried away the private sounds of my grief.

"What do you know of Charis?" I breathed.

"How *could* you know?"

He took the cup from my shaking hand and set it on the table. "I know that Zeus takes what he wants, always. I know what he did to her, that he broke your heart." His eyes were downcast, and when he raised them, they burned with a fierce light. "I, too, have cried out against his violence, Persephone. You are not alone." His expression softened. "In myself, you have a friend."

"A friend?"

"Yes." He offered his hand once more, and I accepted it, tentatively placing my fingers in his flickering palm. He grasped hard and all but dragged me out beyond two sky-grazing columns. We stood on a narrow balcony, and, far below, the earth turned, blue-green and shining. It was so beautiful, the melding of living colors. Now, at this moment, so many mortals were living out their lives on that spinning orb. So much heartache and love and hardship and life. I leaned on the balcony railing and stared down, awestruck.

"Zeus has taken much from me. I have learned to live with loss. A worthy existence is still possible." Hermes turned to me, elbows on the railing, eyes searching my face. "But you do not have to let *them*"—he tossed a sour glance over his shoulder—"dictate how things must be, Persephone."

These words—it was as if he knew my heart. I opened my mouth and closed it, tears brimming at the corners of my eyes. I could not weep again, not here, not on Olympus. "My path is set," I whispered, threading my fingers together, like the pattern of my life. "I am the daughter of Zeus, and I am, therefore, an Olympian, with all that entails." I shook my head helplessly. "I have lost my love. I feel so empty. I don't know what to do."

For a long moment, I thought he was laughing, and he was, but his mouth hung open like a water-starved animal, and he leaned close, lips curving up as he spoke a single word, the dare, the key: "Rebel."

Rebel.

As if I could, as if it were possible.

"It is." His eyes were on fire, shining so brightly, and for the first time in a month, I felt my heart shift to something other than sadness. A glimmer of hope shone from deep within me, beneath the rubble of my broken heart.

"Can you hear what I'm thinking?" I whispered, and he surprised me by nodding.

"Not everything. Mostly, I sense feelings. It's a lucky gift to have." He shimmered momentarily, flickered out, and then reappeared with a bunch of grapes in his hand. He began to pluck them, one by one, and tossed them into his mouth, all the while regarding me with his too-wide grin.

"I have wished I could do something, go somewhere, to get away from all of this." I waved a hand at the crowd behind us. "But there is nowhere on the earth that is not my mother's domain, and my mother fears Zeus." My voice caught, and I coughed into my hand. "I fear Zeus, too."

"Oh, sweet, sweet Persephone," said Hermes, leaning closer, as if we were sharing a secret. "Our father is violent, selfish, and he exists for no other purpose than his own satiation. You say that your mother fears Zeus, and that you fear Zeus. You want to escape all of this but don't have anyplace to go."

Hermes shimmered and appeared at once on the other side of me. "You say that all the earth is your mother's domain."

"It is," I replied, perplexed. "Any child knows this."

"All that is *on the earth*." He lifted his eyebrows, staring intensely at me.

I crossed my arms over my chest. "Yes, yes, of course."

"But…" He chewed a grape, then another. "Not what is under it."

"What do you—under—"

"Persephone!"

Even as I felt my mother's cool fingers grasp my arm, felt her tug me through the columns, heard her haze of chatter, Hermes' words pulsed within me. I walked in a fog. I staggered, glanced at Hermes, open-mouthed, and—slowly, deliberately—he winked, blew me a kiss.

And disappeared.

"Persephone, are you listening to me?" Demeter exclaimed, shoving some stray locks back from her pale forehead, patting my hand and rubbing it hard, too hard—her nervous habit.

I should have noticed the tremor in her voice, but it wasn't until he stepped within my line of sight, and I blinked, once, twice, that I realized what had happened, what was about to happen.

"Dear, I want you to meet your father, officially." She inhaled deeply, and I stared at her, at the way the fabric of her gown quivered in the space over her heart. "Persephone, this is Zeus."

Fear and anger bubbled down my spine as I looked up, up, up at the shining countenance of the king of all the gods. Zeus. Zeus, who had destroyed my life.

Zeus, my father.

"She is beautiful," he boomed in syllables like crashing bells. They rung across the palace, reverberating again and again, so that conversations paused, words clipped, and every god and goddess pressed forward to see who Zeus complimented. He took my hand and kissed it, and the only thing I knew was his lips were wet, and I stared too long at the mark they left on my skin. I shivered, hid my hand away, and his great silver brows raised. He inhaled as if to speak, but my mother stepped between us. I gaped at her hand on his wrist, petting the shining hairs there.

"She looks like you, Demeter." Zeus held his arms wide, face beaming. "Welcome to Olympus, my daughter!"

I shrunk into myself, wished I could shimmer and go, fast as Hermes.

But I couldn't, and my father gathered me into an embrace so tight that the breath left me, and dark circles spun before my eyes. He was laughing—oh, I *knew* that laugh, and I felt it like a kick to my stomach. My hands drew into fists.

He'd laughed when he was done with Charis.

I hated him so much in that moment that I didn't know what to do.

It was instinct, the struggle out of his grasp, how I lost myself easily in the crowd. I slipped back between the columns on the balcony and waited for a long moment in the small space between marble and railing and never-ending blackness and stars. My heart pounded, and my ears buzzed, and I didn't know what to think or how to feel. Hermes said "rebel," as if it were a simple thing to thwart Zeus, to escape his infinite reach and power. How could I? It was impossible, everything was impossible, and I was so tired, so angry, so sad.

I rubbed my eyes and stared down at the revolving, shimmering globe. From here, it seemed a pebble that I might cradle in my hand. Tiny. So vulnerable.

There was nothing I could do. I was trapped.

Neither Zeus nor Demeter came looking for me, and it was just as well. If I'd offended him, if I'd angered him, I would fall to his wrath soon enough, wouldn't I? I dropped my head into my hands.

There was laughter just behind the column, and despite myself, I turned to look, peeking around the marble edge.

I had met Athena once, when she visited my mother. I remember thinking she had laughed a great deal for someone rumored so somber, and she had kissed my mother very tenderly goodbye. Here, now, her jet-black curls were swept up beneath a glittering circlet, and she draped an arm about a mortal girl's shoulder. A goblet appeared between them, and Athena drank deeply, tilting her head back until the goblet was emptied. She tossed it over her shoulder, and quick as a hawk, she drew her companion's smiling mouth down for a kiss.

I watched, bewitched, breathless, heart pounding out a rhythm I had almost forgotten. Athena and the girl broke apart for air, laughing, arms entangled together. I blushed; my skin felt slick. I breathed in and out and ducked back to my hiding place behind the column, on the balcony hanging over the earth.

Charis.

I dug my nails into my palms and concentrated on breathing.

It was not sudden, how the room behind me grew dark, throwing long shadows from the torchlight upon the balcony floor. It was a gradual thing, and I almost failed to notice it, but for the silence. No one laughed or spoke; there was no clink of goblet or twang of lyre. Everything, everything fell to a silence that crawled into my ears and roared.

I shook my head, straightened, peered again around the column at the great room. All throughout the palace, a deep quiet crept, cold as a chill. I saw the gods and goddesses shudder, and then the darkness fell like a curtain, became complete. The stars themselves were blotted out for three terrible heartbeats.

There was the sound of footsteps upon the marble, and the light returned.

"Hades has come." I heard the whisper— Athena's whisper—and I started. Hades? I stood on the tips of my toes, trying to catch a glimpse.

All of us there had been touched by Zeus' cruelty, in some form or another. We were meaningless to him, toys to be played with and tossed. But the story of Zeus's ultimate betrayal was well known.

Zeus and Poseidon and Hades were created from the earth in the time before time—the time of the Titans. They cast lots to determine which of them would rule the kingdom of the sea, the kingdom of the dead, and the kingdom of the sky. Poseidon and Zeus chose the longest straws, so Hades was left with no choice but to reign over the kingdom of the dead, the Underworld.

It did not come to light until later that Zeus had fixed the proceedings to make certain he would get his way—to become ruler of the greatest kingdom, as well as all of the gods. He would never have risked a fair game of chance. Could never have hidden away his splendor in that world of endless darkness.

I shivered, wrapping my arms about my middle. Hades rarely appeared at Olympus, choosing to spend his time, instead, sequestered away in that place of shadows, alone.

My eyes searched the murmuring crowd. Though I was uncertain as to Hades' appearance, I assumed I would recognize the god of the Underworld when I saw him.

But where was he? Over there were Poseidon and Athena, whispering behind their hands. I saw Artemis and Apollo break apart as Zeus moved between them, climbed several high steps and staggered into his towering throne, hefting his goblet of ambrosia aloft.

"Persephone." I jumped, heart racing, and Hermes grinned down at me, his face a handbreadth from my own.

"You have a habit of startling me," I whispered to him, but he shook his head, pressed a finger to his lips. My brow furrowed as he took my hand and led me out onto the floor of the great room, to linger again amidst the gods. I felt naked, misplaced, but Hermes stood behind me and elbowed me forward. I yielded and stumbled a step, two steps. Finally, my frustration rising, I turned to admonish him but paused mid-motion because—I had run into someone.

Life slowed, slowed, slowed. I muttered, "Excuse me," looked up at the woman I did not recognize, had never before seen, my heart slack until it thundered in one gigantic leap against my bones.

Everything stopped.

Her eyes were black, every part of them, her skin pale, like milk. Her hair dropped to the small of her back, night-colored curls that shone, smooth and liquid, as she cocked her head, as she gazed down at me without a change of expression. She wasn't beautiful—the lines of her jaw, her nose, were too proud, too sharp and straight. But she was mesmerizing, like a whirlpool of dark water, where secrets lurked.

I looked up at her, and I was lost in the black of her eyes, and I did not see her take my hand, but I felt her hold it, as if it were meant to be in the cage of her fingers, gently cradled.

"Hello," she said, her voice softer than a whisper. I blinked once, twice, trying to shake the feeling I had heard her speak before—perhaps in a dream.

And then, "I am Hades," she said.

My world fell away.

Hades…Hades, the lord of the underworld…was a woman.

"But, but…" I spluttered, and she watched me with catlike curiosity, head tilted to the sound of my voice as I attempted to regain my senses. "They call you the lord of the Underworld. I thought—"

"It is a slur," she breathed. I had to lean forward to hear her words. Her face remained still, placid, as if she were wearing a mask.

I didn't know what to say—that I was sheltered? Should I apologize that I hadn't known? She still held my hand, fingers curled into my palm like a vine. "I'm sorry," I managed. There was nothing else within me, and the moment stretched on into an eternity as my heart beat against the door of my chest.

I'd forgotten Hermes was there, and he cleared his throat now, stepping alongside us, staring down at our hands, together.

"Hades," he murmured, chin inclined, smile twisting up and up. "It's begun, now that you've met her."

"What?" My head spun; everything was happening too fast. Her eyes had never once left mine, two dark stars pulling me in. My blood pounded fast and hot, and I didn't understand what was happening, but my body did. No, she was not beautiful, but she didn't need to be. I was drawn to her, bewitched by her, a plant angling up to drink in her sun. Still, still, she had not let go of my hand.

"Hermes, may I have a moment with her?" she asked, turning toward him. When her eyes moved away, I felt an emptiness, a hollow, a great, dark ache.

Hermes frowned, shook his head once, twice, and shimmered into nothingness.

She raised my hand, then, so slowly that I held my breath until her lips pressed against my skin, warmer than I'd imagined, and soft. Something within me shattered as she swallowed me up again with her dark eyes, said: "You are lovely, Persephone."

I stared down at her bent head, spellbound. "Thank you," I whispered. She rose.

Where Zeus's lips had been wet, rough, pushing hard enough against my hand to leave a bruise…she was the opposite—gentle. Yet I felt her everywhere. I shivered, closed my eyes. She did not let go of my hand but turned it over, tracing the line of my palm with her thumb.

"It has been a deep honor, meeting you, seeing you. You defy my imaginings." A small smile played over her mouth as she shook her head, traced her fingers against the hollow of my hand. "I hope to see you again."

She looked as if she might say more—she looked hopeful—but something changed, and her eyes flickered. She sighed, pressed her lips together, squeezed my hand. Hades turned and disappeared into the crowd of Olympians.

"No—" I put my hand over my heart, breathed in and out.

"In front of all the others." Hermes was shimmering beside me, leaning close; he shook his head. "She's either stupid or very brave."

I felt as if I were waking from a very long sleep. I stared at the floor, wondering what was real, what was a dream. "I don't understand. That…she was Hades?"

"In the death," he snickered, and he held up his goblet of ambrosia to me, as if in a toast. "It has begun."

"I don't understand…"

"You'd better start understanding, and fast, little girl." Hermes laughed at me, grinning wickedly. Quick as a blink, he grabbed my hand and turned it over. Where Hades had kissed me, where her skin had touched my own, was the lightest dusting of gold. It glittered now, beneath the light of the stars.

"You, Persephone, Demeter's daughter, daughter of Zeus…you will have choices to make. Very soon." I could smell the sickly sweet ambrosia wafting from his mouth. "Everything that will be, or could be, is dependent upon what you choose to do," he told me. "*You must choose wisely.*"

"But why—"

He draped an arm about the shoulders of Artemis, who had just moved near, her brother at her side. Both stared at me with apologetic smiles.

As one, Hermes, Apollo and Artemis turned toward the ambrosia-laden tables, speaking to each other in hushed voices, and I cherished the moment, the moment I'd been seeking all the night long, to be alone.

I watched my hand, watched the gold dust sparkle. Above, beyond the columns of the titanic Olympian Palace, the stars still shone and sang.

Was I enchanted? For the remainder of the night, no one spoke to me, touched me. I hadn't even met Hebe, Hera's daughter. Along with Harmonia, she was my rival, according to my mother. Rival for what? It all seemed so absurd, so irrelevant. All of this opulence, this false camaraderie.

I sat outside of the palace and stared down at my lap and willed, wished, that Hades would find me. This was the only entrance, the only exit. Surely, sooner or later, she would come. Perhaps she would take my hand again. Ornament me with her dust of gold.

But she did not come. At the end, when gods

were strewn about the floor, ambrosia so thick that
my sandals stuck with each step, I wandered,
cautious, until I found Zeus unconscious and spent,
sprawled, one leg dangling over the arm of his throne.
I was safe. For now.

Hades was not there.

I woke my mother, drew her up, helped her
into her chariot of cows that trundled us down,
through the heavens, back to our beckoning earth.

Through the warm air, through the forest,
back in the bower, my lifelong home, I moved
without seeing, lay down and stared.

I was bewitched. I could think of nothing but
the goddess of the dead.

Two: Visitation

"To be honest, I don't remember much about last night." Demeter smiled softly, shook her head. "But it wasn't terrible—was it terrible? Zeus was favorable toward you, I think."

We stood together in the bower, late morning sunshine bright and shafted, lancing through the green leaves and grapevines. The air smelled heady, of warm earth and sweet fruits, but when I took one of the grapes in my mouth, it tasted bitter.

"It wasn't terrible." I held my tongue in regard to Zeus. My mother knew how much I hated him. But there was one topic I must broach. "Hades," I whispered, startling myself by speaking her name here, aloud. Our encounter, the words we shared only hours ago—they seemed like a secret, a secret all my own, and I was protective of them. "She's a woman.

You never told me that."

Demeter sighed, sat down on an accommodating swell of greenery. She spread her hands, studied my face. "It never mattered, Persephone. I wasn't hiding it from you."

"I didn't say you were." I smoothed my tunic beneath me and sat opposite her, my eyes drawn down to the ground. "Is Zeus...cruel to her?" I didn't want to know that he was, but, still, I needed to ask.

"Oh..." My mother exhaled once more, patted the space above my knee. "He taunts her. Calls her the 'lord' of the dead because she favors the company of women. She is not like him, or Poseidon. Hades is good."

My lips parted, surprised. "Are you familiar with her, then?"

"Oh..." She hesitated. "No, no one is, not really. Except, I suppose, for the dead. But that's too somber a subject for a golden morning, the morning after your debut. I am so proud of you, my Persephone." She held out her arms to me, and I felt like a little girl again as I ducked my head against her shoulder. But I did not feel the old comfort blossom inside my heart when she held me in her arms. She was trembling a little.

"Speaking...of Zeus..." she spoke haltingly into my hair, pausing for a long moment during which neither of us moved—or breathed. "Since he was unable to talk long with you last night, he hoped to remedy that..." She strung the stilted words together like red berries on a poison tree. I arched back from her in horror.

There was such sadness in her eyes.

"He is coming down later today so that he

may bless you, acquaint himself with you."

"*Here*," I whispered. "Zeus is coming here?"

"Persephone, I couldn't dissuade him. I tried—please believe me, I tried. Once he gets an idea in his head…" She looked so small, so defeated.

I found my feet, cleared my throat, closed my eyes as my mother's fears collided with my own. "I'm sorry, but I won't be here when he comes—I *can't* be. I'd do something wrong. I'd make him angry with me. With you."

My mother was nodding, her lovely face pale.

"That may be best," she whispered, petting the blue morning glory vine curling like a puppy in her lap. "I'll…I'll think of an excuse for you. It will be all right. It will." She sounded unconvinced, and her eyes shone like moons. "I'm sorry, Persephone."

I stood for a moment, disarmed, as I gazed down at my mother, my mother who would lie to the king of all the gods for me, for *me*. My mother. After Charis, I had doubted her. But I knew, had always known, the depth of her love for me, deeper than the deepest roots, deeper than the Underworld itself. Words crowded my throat; I could say them, could say anything, but words would never be enough, truly.

She rose, smooth and tall and serene. I could not help her, could not save her. I could not save myself.

My heart splintered, and I needed to leave, needed to escape her kindness and her courage, her trembling hands, the fear buried behind the calm of her eyes. So, slowly, I kissed my mother on her cool cheek and turned and left, vines catching at my hair.

Under the pink clouds, beneath the hum of

growing things, I cursed myself, balled my fists. I felt like a coward and a traitor. I should have stayed. But to engage in a father-daughter meeting with Zeus? My skin chilled at the thought.

I don't remember how I moved through the forest—I must have run, though, because my legs were bleeding the blue blood of the immortals. It pooled on my briar-torn shins, and I stumbled and fell, over and over. I didn't know where to go. The nymphs stared at me when I passed them. They must have thought me mad. I just wanted to be alone, left alone, safe in a new world, where Zeus could never come. An idea woke in my heart then, and I followed the curve of the sun in the sky, creating my own path through the overgrown woods.

Finally, the trees fell away, the ground softened beneath my feet, and I threw myself toward the sea.

My legs could not carry me fast enough. I ran through the dunes, kicking up a fog of sand. I felt a rhythm within me: the crashing of the waves, the crashing of my heartbeat. I fell down upon the hot sand, sunk my hands deep into the damp, golden crumbles of it, and sobbed—wet, heaving sobs—for the hopelessness, the unfairness, the prison in my mother's eyes. I sobbed as the wind sang through the sea grasses, as the surf crested, spilled, water removing earth, water sweeping it all away.

Through tear-filled eyes, I gazed at the endless blue of the ocean. I had been here a few times but not many. My mother had taken me here once, when I was very small, to play with the sea nymphs. Their laughter had been strange but sweet, kind. They had made me a necklace of pearls, had called it the hearts of oysters. They'd shown me an oyster, then, tickled him so that he smiled at me, so I could see the hard shining pearl lying within. My mother and I had laughed, and the sun had gleamed like a polished yellow stone, and all I knew was joy.

I stood up, dusted the sand from my tunic, moved nearer to the sea. The surf pounded against the earth, over and over, and it was so loud and still so comforting, a roaring hush that silenced my heart.

When Zeus arrived, found me missing, he would command my mother to find me. And she would have no choice but to ask her flowers, her trees, her vines and grasses where I'd hidden myself, and—traitors all—they would bend and shift, recreate my trail. I would be caught as swiftly as a rabbit in the mouth of a fox.

And when I was dragged before Zeus, I would spit on him. I would scream and sob. I would say, "You have taken away the only person who meant anything to me." I would say, "Why does my mother fear you so much? What have you done to her?" And he would regard me with that smug twist to his lips and laugh until his sides were sore, while my mother's hands shook, while she shrunk smaller and smaller in his electric shadow. Then he would punish me in some clever way—perhaps I'd become a rosebush like Charis, or a mirror pool, or a monstrous creature that no mother or sweet nymph could ever love—and I would be lost forever.

I would speak the truth, but it wouldn't make a difference. Zeus would be the same as before, my mother the same, cowering before him, and the pattern would repeat itself over and over and over again. There was nothing I could do to stop it.

Nothing.

I made my way down to the seawater, felt it wash over my feet, cooling me, and I closed my eyes and held my face up to the light. I was weary: world weary, bone weary. I wanted my halcyon days back, those too-few days of laughing in the sunshine hand-in-hand with my beloved, of feeling her warmth beside me as night fell and the stars peeked out. I was so innocent then to the pain in the world, the pain a cruel father could cause. The pain of hearts ripped in half.

I wanted my life to be beautiful again. No matter what foul things lurked in my future, that future Zeus and my mother intended for me, could I hold onto the shining, lovely past, when this, all of this, became too difficult to bear? Would I always remember that, once, my life *had* been beautiful, that I had experienced—felt, touched—beauty? Could that alone sustain me for an immortal's lifetime? I was so young. I had experienced so little, in the grand scheme of forever. Could the memory of that handful of months, drawn thin and threadbare over the centuries, be enough?

"Demeter's daughter…"

The words were so soft, at first, that I almost didn't hear them over the crash of the sea.   But they came again, like music: "Demeter's daughter…"

Lovely—so lovely. They rode the waves up and down, their long green hair braided with pearls or swept up with coral combs. Their eyes were milky and wet, smooth spongy skin white as the bellies of sharks. My old friends. The sea nymphs.

"You remember me?" I murmured, holding out my hands. "It's been so long…"

They came ashore one by one, a stream of lithe ladies with haunting, slippery smiles. They embraced me, kissed me, whispered in my ears, and when they laughed, it was the sound of tide breaking.

"We never forget, Demeter's daughter. We have missed you."

I stepped into the water with them, and they held me up, like a queen in a chair.

When I was small, they filled my hands with broken bits of water-smoothed pottery, iridescent shells, and other mysteries of the deep. They did so again, heaping shining, strange things upon me; soon my palms overflowed with wet, glistening treasure.

"Thank you," I whispered, and I carried it all back to the shore. Making a little hollow in the hot sand, I buried the tokens.

The wet skin along my back prickled, and I stood, brushing coarse sand from my hands and arms. The wind was picking up, and the water crashed harder against the sand and rocks, over and over, as if—by pounding the earth—it could shape the dirt, the stone, to something new, something more like itself, liquid and lucid and changing. I stooped and gathered a handful of ocean. The sea nymphs, quiet now, watched me with unblinking white eyes. It had been so many years since I had seen them last, but they remembered me. How much longer would it take them to forget me? For the world to forget me?

"Persephone..." The sea nymph brushed webbed fingers against the cool skin of my leg. I shuddered, though the sensation was not unpleasant, only surprising.

"We do not have flowers in the ocean," she whispered to me. "Persephone, will you gather flowers for us? We so love beautiful things, and they are the most beautiful of all. If you pick us flowers, we will weave crowns for ourselves, and for you. We will all be lovely together." Again, her hand on my leg. "Oh, pick us flowers, Persephone!"

It was a simple wish to grant. Water streamed over my body as I moved out of the ocean, and I hitched up my drenched tunic to my thighs. Footprints trailed behind me to the water's edge, as if I had just risen from a shell, new-created in the frothing secrets of the deep.

There was a flower near the shoreline, choked by sea grasses. It was white and plain, not the loveliest of my mother's kingdom, but I admired its stubbornness, sprouting here in the sand, so far from its native ground.

What would happen to me after this stolen hour? I couldn't think of it. I couldn't.

I found a patch of violets and plucked one of the little purple blooms.

What would Zeus say to me? Would he even remember Charis?

I plucked another flower.

Hades had kissed my hand…this hand. She had sprinkled it in gold dust. I plucked another flower and gazed down at my fingers. There was still the shimmer of gold upon them. I wanted it there always. Always.

I plucked another flower.

"Rebel," Hermes had told me.

I plucked another flower.

Soon, my skirt was filled with petals and leaves, fragrant with sweet, sun-warmed perfumes. I held the gathered fabric tight in my hands, flowers grazing against my arms, my fingers, soft as skin. Flower and flower I gathered, as if under a spell. Finally, languorous, awake from a dream, I raised my heavy-lidded eyes.

I was in an unfamiliar valley, a round bowl of earth with trees edging its rim, cupping the grass and wildflowers that flourished down and within. I paused near the bottom, petals fluttering from my skirt, and turned to go. I had wandered too far in my enchanted searching; I no longer heard the cresting of the sea.

I took a few steps backward, and then I saw it.

It was red, bright red, red like mortals' blood. I watched it move, back and forth, borne up on a wind I could not feel. It enticed me.

I needed this flower. I needed to take it.

As I stepped forward, I felt the earth shift beneath my feet like sand, but still I reached, wrapped my glittering hand around the flower's stem. Its petals were thin, like parchment.

I plucked it, brought it to my nose, breathed the scent of it: sweet but faint as dusk light.

I breathed it in again and felt the ground give way.

I rolled and fell in a rain of flowers. The earth shook like a wild mare, desperate to be rid of me, and I cried out, clinging first to a jagged bush, then a broken root. I slipped, let go, screamed, certain I would be swallowed down like a grape by my own earth, my mother's earth. Would she know? Would she find me, buried so deep? Or would I be lost and aware for all time—an immortal seed, never growing?

But then it stopped—the breaking, the shifting.

It stopped.

And I breathed in and out and coughed a cloud of dust.

The dust was multicolored and separated into shafts of light from the lowering sun. I stood, or tried to, and grimaced when I saw how my right ankle twisted beneath me. Gods are not impervious—it would take an hour or more to heal the bone's break. I sank down and picked crushed petals from my skirt, the red flower long gone, and forgotten.

I knew of quakes, had experienced them before: the earth rears up and moves like an animal, impossible to seat.

But this had been different somehow…and strange.

The dust began to clear as I sat waiting, impatient. Darkness had amassed in the center of the valley, and as my eyes made sense of it, I made out a gigantic, gaping hole carved into the earth. It was as wide as the gates of Olympus and had *not* been there before. I rose and steadied myself against an outcropping of rocks, waiting, watching.

I heard it before I saw it rise out of the maw, before I saw the twisting metal and the sparking hooves. It came as a rumble of thunder, and up through the hole burst two wild black horses in harness—and behind them, a heavy chariot, dark as the night sky.

At the helm stood Hades.

I sank down to my knees, felt my ankle turn painfully beneath me, as the horses reared, as they screamed into the darkening sky, tossing their heads like monsters. When the chariot settled on the earth, Hades jumped down and placed a hand on each of the beast's necks, whispered softly to them, so that they pricked their black ears in her direction, gentled, stood straight and quiet. She smiled with such fondness.

From the chariot floor, Hades gathered a faint, dark wisp, coiled like rope. It uncoiled when she touched it, long and thin, snakelike. It shimmered in the struggling light as she gathered it close to her chest, as gentle as a mother. She spoke a few faint words that I could not hear, and she lifted her hands over her head. The wisp spiraled up into the sky and began an ascent toward the dome of the heavens. It glittered, winked in and out of sight, and was gone.

Hades watched the sky for a long moment, while I watched her.

When she lowered her gaze, took in the destruction of the valley with her eyes, she took me in, too: crumpled on the broken ground, dead flowers my companions.

Her face, as before, was a mask of white marble, unreadable, but for a single instant, her mask cracked, and I saw—surprise? Excitement? I couldn't tell for certain, but she took a step toward me, waving her hand.

"Persephone," she said, her voice whisper-soft. "Why—why are you here?"

"I was…gathering flowers." I blushed, feeling childish, and gestured lamely at the crushed petals on the valley floor. She gazed down at the headless stems and flattened flowers, uncomprehending.

"Gathering flowers," she repeated.

"For crowns." I bit off the words, staggered to my feet and turned to go, limping, but she stayed me, stepping forward and wrapping her fingers about my wrist. I jumped, startled.

"Forgive me," she whispered, but she did not let go, her fingers yielding and gentle on my skin. Here, standing so close to one another, and so removed from the over-perfumed mob of Olympians, I breathed in her scent, and it soothed me. She smelled of the earth—good, kind earth—and of hidden pools of black water, deep-growing things. Dark, familiar.

I chewed my lip as she stared down at my ankle, as her brows drew together and her eyes filled with concern. "My arrival injured you."

I shook my head. "I'll heal." But she was kneeling down, touching the swollen circumference of my ankle—so gently, like the wing-flutter of a moth.

Without a word, Hades stood, turned from me and moved back to her chariot. I watched, mystified, as she opened the waist-high door, reached down and in and retrieved a rough-hewn box. She hurried back with it, knelt down at my feet again.

"This won't hurt, I promise," she said. From the box, she withdrew the smallest of glass flasks, carefully removed the seal, and a dark gathering of liquid, black as ink and cold, dripped from the bottle onto my ankle.

I watched, mesmerized, as, within ten flutters of my eyelids, my bruised skin regained its regular hue, the swelling deflated. I put my weight on my ankle, and it offered no complaint.

"Remarkable," I breathed.

Hades stopped up the flask and put it back in her box, smiling.

I held my breath, peering down at the goddess of the Underworld. I had been wrong before. She *was* beautiful. I felt my awareness of her beauty like a pain, and I feared she would notice, would ask me what was the matter, so I cleared my throat, rubbed at my eyes, grasped for plain words to break this spell.

I said, "What was that? That liquid?"

"A single drop from the river Lethe, a river of my kingdom. Its waters steep with forgetfulness, oblivion. So that drop—" She gestured at my repaired ankle. "It made the bone forget it was broken."

"Ah, clever!"

She rose, holding her box beneath her arm, and again she smiled. It was a small, shy smile, unassuming. I had never met another god or goddess with so gentle a manner. I stared at her, and I was not sorry for it.

"Thank you," I murmured. "You are very kind."

She shrugged; the stone mask again fell over her features. I felt a pang deep as an old root. I watched her as she moved back to her chariot, the box in her arms. "As you said, your ankle would have healed on its own. I simply quickened the process. It was through my carelessness that it happened at all."

"Is this…is this how you always come up from the Underworld?" I was grappling for words. I wanted to speak with her longer, *keep* her longer, if I could. Like a pup, I followed after her to the chariot; she stepped up and in. I placed my fingers gently upon the dark carved rim, as if, by holding my hands there, I could hold her.

"No," she told me. "I rarely rise to the surface. The true door to the Underworld is deep in the heart of the Immortals Forest." Hades waved toward the trees, toward my home. "But it is long to travel, and I had an urgent matter." She grimaced.

"Urgent?" I remembered the snaking wisp, how gently she had guided it to the sky.

"A soul came down to my kingdom by mistake—it wasn't his time to die. So I brought him back."

"You journeyed all this way for a mortal's soul?" I could not hide my astonishment. I had had little interaction with humans, but gods generally viewed the mortals with varying amounts of contempt or indifference. There were a few, like my mother, who loved their worshippers, but not many, to my knowledge, and certainly none who would have undertaken such a voyage, from the Underworld to the face of the earth, for the good of a single soul.

"Of course," said Hades, and repeated, "It wasn't his time."

We stared at one another for a long moment. I smiled.

"That was kind of you," I said, finally, weakly, because I couldn't find words true enough to convey the depth of my admiration.

She had been gathering up the reins but paused now, lowering them back to the rim of the chariot. She reached down and took one of my hands, bent her head and brushed her lips against my palm.

My hand was streaked with earth and yellow pollen, and I wanted to steal it back from her, ashamed, but I couldn't bring myself to break this connection. Her face rose before me, her black eyes bright.

I gazed into those eyes, wondering what thoughts brewed behind them.

She was silhouetted by the clouds, by the

glow of the sun above the bowl of the valley, orange and red, a disharmony of brilliance against the paleness of her skin, the limitless darkness of her stare.

"Zeus is coming to see me today." My words surprised me; I hadn't meant to speak them. But I felt so safe. Hades had been kind to a mortal, and I was hungry for kindness. So—haltingly, head bowed—I told my story. I told her of Charis and Zeus, of my mother's plans for me. I told her that Zeus meant to bless me, and that I desired nothing he had to offer.

I told her that I had no place to go.

When I finished my tale, I did not feel better, but there was something new and clear amid the shadows within me, and I recognized it with gratitude: relief.

Hades had not spoken a word since I began. She had simply listened. But she opened her mouth now, dark eyes shining, and a single tear traced down her cheek. It fell on my hand, glittered there. "I am so very sorry, Persephone."

Her tear in my palm—it seemed a precious thing.

I was exhausted, spent, but I nodded my thanks and turned to go. Someone else knew now, knew of Zeus' travesty, Charis' tragedy, and that was enough.

"Wait."

Hades tugged at my hand, and I felt the pulse of her heart there.

"Do you believe in coincidence, Persephone?" She bent her head down, and I tilted mine up. Again, that scent: dark, never-known places; smooth water; earth secrets. She did not wait for me to respond—I did not know *how* to respond—but continued, "I don't believe that paths cross by chance. I don't believe that two people who were foretold to join fates could, randomly, stumble upon one another a day after their first meeting…"

Foretold? My heart thundered as she spoke, even as she kept her voice soft, whispered.

"Persephone," she said, never once pulling her eyes from mine; the intensity within them startled me. "I can help you."

"But…how? There is no way to—Zeus—"

"Will you come with me, down to the Underworld?"

My heart caught, ceased to beat for a breath. And another.

"Come to my kingdom," Hades said, "and you will be free."

I gasped. "Hades—"

The implications of the choice she offered me weighted my heart. Did I want this? Could I leave my mother? My forest? Is this what Hermes meant, to rebel? I could not be found under the earth; Zeus would not touch me there. It *must* have been what Hermes had in mind. But how had he known?

I didn't know what to do, and my heart fluttered against my ribs, caught and cornered.

The burdens of the day seemed flimsy now, dissolved, as I recognized in this choice the first true choice I had been given in my whole life. It was sacred to me, a new, young thing, and I held it as carefully as a nestling.

"Hades," I said again, and looked deep into her eyes, her limitless eyes, and I wanted to fall into them. I wanted to fall into the earth with her.

But then I remembered my mother's trembling hands.

"I don't know what to do. Can I have some time to consider this?"

I feared she would say no. I feared she would flick the reins, and the world would swallow up her body and her beasts, and she would be gone from me, leaving behind only her scent and the ghost of her hand in mine.

But she stayed.

She straightened her back and inclined her head to me. "Of course. Forgive my forwardness. I feel your pain and can't bear it. Any aid I may offer you, Persephone, I give it freely."

I closed my eyes as she brushed her lips to my palm. Even in the sallow light, I saw the sprinkling of gold dust, like a tattoo marking the places her body touched mine. Now she gathered the reins in her hands, and the horses trembled, anticipating their great descent. They held their black heads high, eyes rolling.

"I'll await your answer," Hades said, and I moved my hand to my heart.

"Thank you." I ventured a small, sad smile. "My mother was right about you."

She tilted her head, raised a brow. "Demeter spoke of me?"

"She said that you're different. That you're good. You are good to me."

Something like amusement curled the line of her mouth. "If you'll let me be, Persephone," she whispered, so quietly that I had to lean closer to catch her words, "I will be even better."

I pressed my fingers to my lips.

Her words lingered between us as she raised her hand to me in parting. The horses bellowed and reared, the chariot shuddered, and the entire shadowy assemblage leapt into the gaping pit before me, swallowed whole. The horses' screams echoed long after the animals, and Hades, had disappeared.

The ground moved beneath me, but calmer this time, and the great mouth cut into the earth sewed itself up, as if by an invisible seamstress.

Dazed, I climbed out of the valley, sought the ocean again. *Move forward*, I commanded myself. *Don't look back.*

I gathered a handful of flowers and carried them to the sea nymphs.

They wove me a crown, as they'd promised, and I wore it, accepted their flattery and hugs, but my heart was lost in a place to which I'd never traveled. The nymphs tried to fetch me back; they sang me sea songs, stroked my arms with their hands smooth as shells. The water splashed over my legs, and I tasted salt on my lips.

I turned to go.

"Stay awhile," they pleaded. "Demeter's daughter, please."

"I must go home," I told them, and left, the stars shining the way.

Three: Taken

Zeus did not come that day, or the next or the next. Demeter fretted and paced the bower. Worry made her careless, so that her flowers sprouted strange and poison fruits, and her vines tangled into impossible knots. I stayed away, took refuge in the Immortals Forest.

I found a hollow in an old, forgiving tree, curled up within it, and hoarded my thoughts like acorns.

"You are distracted," my mother's nymphs whispered to me, pulling at my hands, my garments. They were worried about me—they knew who my father was. They knew Zeus would come, sooner or later. Perhaps they knew more than I did, for a few wept and hid their faces when they saw me. I tried to keep to myself, discovering other hidden nooks—

places to sit alone with my conflicted heart.

On the fourth day, he came.

I walked into the bower to see my mother passionately embracing a stranger.

Zeus.

He stood up straight, tall, too tall for the confines of our little home, but the living walls and ceiling groaned and stretched to accommodate his mass. Zeus wiped the back of his hand over his mouth, and my mother, panting, pulled down her tunic without a word or glance for me.

I glared, silent, as Zeus examined my body with his unfatherly eyes. My stomach roiled with hatred. I clenched my fists at my sides, took a step back for every step he took toward me. We stopped and stood and stared at one another. It was almost comical, and a crazed sort of laughter bubbled up within me, but I suppressed it.

"Demeter's daughter," he intoned wetly. I narrowed my eyes, pushed down with great effort the need within me to deny the title, to tell him, *That is not my name.* The tension between us propagated like the most tenacious weed.

Finally, my mother moved in.

"Say hello to your father, Persephone," she whispered.

I bit my tongue so hard that I tasted blood. I could not speak to him, would not, but he mistook my silence.

"The child's shy, Demeter," he chuckled, reaching for my shoulders. I flinched when his large hands patted my back, caressed the bare skin there, lingering too long. "You have grown up," he said. "Grown up well. And I am impatient to tell you my surprise."

I cast a quick glance at my mother, and her eyes met mine, strangely clear—no, vacant. Her hands trembled so that they blurred along the edges. I inhaled, opened my mouth, but Zeus expelled a laugh so loud that I clamped my hands over my ears, horror-struck. The bower reverberated with the sound: leaves shook on their vines; my heart shook inside my chest.

"We have prepared a place for you on Olympus," he said, grinning, once the noise-quake abated. "You are to come with me, live in my palace on Mount Olympus with the rest of your immortal family." He spread his arms wide, as if he held within them a bounty of gifts for me.

I schooled my features for a long moment, piecing together his words with care, while my mother stood by and watched, my mother with her unblinking eyes, her tears that began to spill, silent truth-tellers, over her cheeks.

"Persephone..." she began, coughing quietly into her hand when her voice broke. "I have sheltered you, sequestered you, because I could not bear to be parted from you. But now you will learn Olympian history and tradition, culture and poise—any number of things that could never be understood fully with me here on the earth."

Listening to her, I could not help but think of the talking birds that repeat overheard phrases without any true sense of their meaning. I knew she meant none of this, believed none of this, wanted none of this for me. I knew her like my own heart. These words were Zeus', not hers.

Still, she said, sadly, "You will be so much

happier on Olympus."

I could not help myself; I laughed.

Demeter shook her head, as if to negate her lies, and put her face in her hands, closed her eyes.

I crept backward to the edge of the bower, felt familiar branches press against my shoulder blades.

I was to become the immortals' plaything. Zeus' shiny new toy. My mother knew this as surely as I did, but how could she stop it? What could she do? In her mind, Zeus was king. Zeus got what he wanted. Zeus had won the game of my life.

More lies.

In reality, Zeus had only made my choice so much simpler.

Fear crawled up my spine, but my tongue was moving before I knew what it would say. "Father," I said, and the word tasted like bile, but I forced civility into my voice. "Please...I must say goodbye. Give me one more night to bid farewell to my mother, my nymphs. I love them all so much, and I would be heartbroken to leave them suddenly."

I had never truly spoken to Zeus before, and he considered me for a long, tense while, as my mother paled, bit her lip, folded and unfolded her hands.

"Very well," he boomed finally. "One night. I'll return tomorrow to fetch you. Until then..." He shimmered in a golden cloud, flashed and was gone.

Gone so completely, I could almost believe he had never been there at all. Except for the stench of ozone burning my nostrils. Except for the miserable expression on my mother's face.

"Persephone..." She looked withered and so lost—Demeter, goddess of all the earth. I shut my eyes, rubbed at my face, tried to slow my catapulting pulse. She gathered me in her arms, and she was crying, and it was all so terrible. My mother smelled of him, of his golden body. His stink made me sick, but I held her tightly.

"I don't know what to do," she whispered, shaking. "I don't know how to save you."

"I do."

I kissed her forehead, twined my fingers with hers. Her eyes asked me questions, but I could offer no answers. What would this desperate act, my choice, mean for her? Would Zeus take vengeance on her? Would he understand—or care—that I had done this of my own free will, that she was not to blame? She couldn't know where I was going, what I was about to do, because I wanted her to remain innocent, beyond reproach.

So I said, "I love you, Mother," and she nodded once, twice. She cupped my face in her hands, questing deep within my eyes as if searching for something. Then she simply turned and left the bower.

I was trembling. I knelt down on the soft, sweet grass of our dwelling, breathing in and out the green perfume.

This was my moment, mine alone.

I remembered the way Hades had taken my hand, wept on my hand.

She was strange and a stranger, and I would follow her down to the land of the dead and darkness. I would give up all I had known for the possibility...

The possibility of what, Persephone?

I bit my lip too hard, breathed in and out and counted my breaths; there was something comforting in the neutrality of numbers.

Freedom.

That was what I wanted. Was there freedom in the Underworld?

Hades was good. I knew that, unquestioning. She held my hand as if it were broken, as if she alone could mend it. She made me feel shining, like a golden thing. There was something deep and dark and so beautiful about her. When I remembered her sad eyes, my heart flipped.

In a life of no choices, this one brash act could set me on a path toward the freedom I longed for more than anything else on—or above—the earth.

"Rebel." I whispered the word and stood, cast my gaze about the bower, stared long at the flowers— so adored and familiar—and the pretty things: candles and precious stones my mother and I had collected over the years we shared together. I knew I would take nothing; there was nothing that I needed. I did not need the beautiful shell comb or the strand of pearls the sea nymphs had given me. I did not need the first flower my mother had ever grown for me, preserved and perfect as the day it bloomed. Perhaps my mother would need it. Perhaps it would comfort her.

I took myself, and I stepped out of the bower, into the Immortals Forest, empty-handed, alone.

I couldn't let my mother see me leave, and I couldn't say goodbye. Already I felt haunted by her hopeless face, her trembling hands. It would be best for both of us if I were to simply vanish, like stars winking out at the break of day.

So I crept along the line of trees and found the great oak. "Farewell," I whispered into her rough bark, wrapped my arms around her great trunk. She had held me from the beginning and until the end.

I suppose that I had always sensed the location of the entrance to the Underworld. It was the one spot that I—and all of the forest inhabitants—evaded, as if by instinct. Now I stole away into the deepest center of the Immortals Forest, those dark thorny paths that I had always skirted, never stepped upon. They were overgrown and eerie, and wide-eyed animals stilled and watched me as if I were a ghost passing through.

The trail twisted and turned beneath gnarled branches that arched over my head, interlocked. I remembered laughing and running with the nymphs, and I remembered the hush that overtook us when we came within feet of these pathways, how we could not force ourselves to enter, could not bear to stay.

Now my heart thundered, and I felt a pushing, something invisible urging me to turn around, go back to my life, back to the light, but I walked on, stubborn and one-minded. The trees around me grew closer and older, and woody vines tripped me at every opportunity.

Gradually, the air began to change. There was a feeling of held breath, of looming greatness, and the tightly laced brambles gave way to an expansive clearing.

I paused.

The surrounding trees cast shadows that flickered over the hard-packed earth, and there, on the far side... As the sun slipped away from the day, and the first star stole into the sky, I saw it: a stony cavity leading down into darkness, wide enough for a chariot and pair of horses. The columns were old, older than I could understand, and the soft gray rock that formed the dome was carved with likenesses of men and gods from the beginning of the world. The beginning of everything. A soft gust of chilled air wended its way out of the opening and teased at my hair, brushed cool fingers over my face. Beckoning me, it seemed.

My eyes moved as if spellbound to the single pomegranate tree thriving alongside the entrance, or, more truly, as part of the entrance itself. The roots and rocks twined together, inseparable, and—as anxiety over my impending descent squeezed my heart and weakened my knees—I reached up and held onto the tree for support.

My fingers stroked the smooth red curve of a fruit. I could tell with a touch that it was ripe, and I tugged it from its branch, held it in my palm, cherishing its comforting weight. It was of my mother's kingdom, yes, but it was of mine, too. And though I had left everything else behind, I tied the pomegranate into a fold of my tunic—food for the journey, I reasoned with myself, but of course I had no need for food. I was simply afraid, and I wanted something I could hold, smell, taste that would remind me of the earth, of growing things, of light. Light makes a pomegranate. I needed to carry some of that light with me, even as I turned my back on it and chose the darkness.

I crossed one foot over the threshold between above and below. There was a vastness before me, and the air made me shiver, but I didn't look back. I couldn't. The skin prickled at the back of my neck, and—one hand on the cool rock of the entrance—I moved forward, picked up my slow, cautious pace to something a bit faster and stepped down, down,

down.

Time passed—how much I could not say—and I was lulled into a thoughtless state, my steady advance as involuntary as my heartbeat. I could see, though just barely. All was cold and quiet until, suddenly, a soft sound startled me. Like sandal on stone. I waited in the darkness, squinting. A shadowy, person-shaped form detached itself from the gloom, swept closer, evolved into the glimmering, shimmering silhouette of a young man with one hand grazing the cool wall.

Hermes. Somehow, he illuminated the space around us with a gentle glow.

"You began without me," he remarked wryly, picking bits of leaves from his tunic. "They never begin without me."

I flinched. "Why are you here?" Fear climbed and clung to my bones. Another god in this forsaken place? Had Zeus sent him? It seemed unlikely, but—

"Don't be foolish." Hermes tapped my forehead and raised a brow. "Hades asked me to fetch you. I'm here to take you to the Underworld."

"I don't need to be taken. I'm already going." I sounded braver than I felt, and his flashing eyes softened.

"Allow me to accompany you, then, Persephone." He could sense my fear, my worry, I was sure. He offered his arm, and I took it with some relief. I was grateful for his presence. The rigidity of my spine eased, and I exhaled a breath I hadn't realized I'd been holding.

Hermes winked at me and pointed a finger at his feet. His sandals sprouted wings—white as doves—and he grabbed me about my waist and hoisted me onto his hip as if I were a child, and we *flew*. My vision warped and flickered. My stomach fell away within me, and I gasped and closed my eyes, buried my face in his shoulder. He laughed. "You're quite safe, I assure you."

And then…only an instant later—

"You can let go," Hermes said, still laughing. I detached my limbs from his body, found solid ground beneath my feet and opened my eyes.

We stood in a narrow cave brightened by wall torches that burned with strange green fire. The space before us stretched away to a pinprick of black; it seemed never-ending. I began to wonder how deep down we were, and the weight of the earth—my earth—seemed to press upon my shoulders, my head. I felt suffocated, so removed from the wide-open spaces and forever sky of my forest. After a few desperate gulps of air, I placed a hand over my heart, willed its beat to steady.

Hermes stamped his feet, and the little wings folded back.

"Are we here?" I asked him. "Is this the Underworld?"

"Almost." He stretched, hands overhead, and then bent forward, shaking out his arms. "I showed off," he confessed, grinning. "It normally takes longer to get here. But you were nervous, and I didn't want to prolong your journey."

"Oh. Thank you."

"It was the least I could do." He smiled at me for a moment. "You've done well, Persephone. And you're nearly there."

"Where are we now?"

He gestured widely. "This is the hall that will

take you to the gateway that will take you to the river that will take you to the Underworld." He nodded toward the endless corridor. "Ever forward. You can't miss it."

We began to walk together, and I counted torches to the rhythm of our sandals scuffing stone. I gave up at two-thousand-forty-three, and we seemed no nearer to…anything.

"I can only take you as far as the gateway," Hermes finally murmured beside me.

"How far is the gateway?"

He pointed.

My face was a handbreadth from a dark metal gate. It hadn't been there a moment ago, I was certain. The sharp-tipped rails were draped in a moss I had never encountered before; it glowed green beneath the torchlight. I touched the iron, hesitant, and it burned my skin, but the gate opened, swinging outward without a creak.

The air here smelled of shadowed water, of forgotten things. Of Hades.

"Well, always nice to see you, Persephone— good luck." Hermes was turning to leave, and I gripped his arm automatically, so tightly he winced.

"Please don't leave me, Hermes," I whispered. "Please."

"You know, you're very pretty when you pout." He was floating above the ground, winged sandals fluttering, and he bent forward to brush a kiss on my cheek. "You must enter the Underworld alone, Persephone. A symbolic journey, if you will."

"But I'm afraid."

He wriggled out of my grasp, drifted down the corridor, the planes of his face shimmering in the ghostly green light.

"Of course you're afraid," his words echoed around me. "This would not be so precious if it came without cost."

"Hermes!"

He disappeared.

I was alone, at the beginning of the Underworld.

I waited.

I don't know why I waited, but I waited—waited for him to come back, to say he had only been teasing me, that of course he would guide me right to Hades' palace—or cave, or whatever sort of abode she dwelled in down here. My faltering bravado had vanished along with my half-brother.

He didn't come back, and at last I felt foolish, just standing there, waiting to be saved.

I bit my lip, turned, and I stepped through the gateway, stepped from rock to more rock, and nothing looked different, but the pull of air was stronger now, cold and luring. It wound round my legs like rope, and I obeyed its tugging, impatient to be done, to be *there*, to see Hades. Soon enough, I began to run.

There was nothing but the unending passage and the cool wind, the green fire, the hard earth under my sore feet. I stopped once or twice, pounded my palms against the craggy walls in frustration, but I didn't consider turning back. If this cave went on forever, I would walk forever.

Then I smelled water.

I almost slipped into the liquid blackness roiling and boiling and licking at my feet, but somehow I caught myself, gripping the edge of the wall with white-knuckled hands. Before me stretched a wide river. I could just make out the shifting waters and, above it all, an unending nothingness of black.

To enter the land of the dead, you must cross the river Styx. I knew this, had heard mention of it here and there, but had never given the mortals' customs concerning death much thought. There were stories of a mysterious boatman, Charon, who exchanged safe passage over the river for golden coins. I had no coins, nothing precious. I felt a rising panic; I would not be able to cross. I would be trapped here at the edge, stuck between two worlds. Nowhere.

Whispers. Distant, hollow whispers. They rose gradually, hushed at first, but soon enough my ears were swept up in a crescendo. The noise surrounded me like the wind, and I was buffeted back and forth by the tiny urgent words. When the last syllables echoed, echoed, faded, and were gone, I felt their absence, feared the silence, and shivered, stealing backward from the lapping water.

He poled across the river on a broken barge that should have sunk but didn't. I couldn't see him, not really: his appearance kept shifting, and one moment he was an old man with a beard, the next a skeleton with bits of flesh dangling between his ribs, the next a small, sad child.

"Welcome to the Underworld," came the whispers, as before, and I realized they were made up of hundreds, thousands of different voices coalesced into one. He/she/it—Charon—held out to me a skin-tangled hand. "Coin for passage."

I recoiled. This was horrible, more horrible than I could have ever imagined. My heart seemed to have stopped beating. My mouth was dry, my tongue useless. I coughed and stuttered, "I have no coin. But Hades invited—"

"It matters not why you are here, only that you are." There was amusement in the lazy susurration. "You must pay me, or you cannot cross."

"What can I give you? What will you take?"

"From one dead beggar, I took an eye." And within the maelstrom of flesh and bone, I found a single blue eye staring out at me, glistening. "From another, I took a heart." I heard the heart beat, too slowly. "What part of your flesh, Persephone, would you offer me that I do not already have in multiples?"

I despaired, thought wildly. My hands pressed against my collarbones, grazed my neck, gathered up fistfuls of night-black hair.

"Will you take this?" The hair pooled in my palms, its bluish sheen shifting so that the light from the torches behind me slid like green oil over its surface. The floating blue eye ogled me, watched as I offered up my hair to the ferryman of the dead.

"Done." It was quick, the cut, though not painless. I touched a hand to my cheek and felt blood gather along the thin slice Charon had made with his blade. He held my fallen locks in one hand, and the whispers rose again, grew louder now, like wails, or keening, but higher, uniting in a single piercing moan. I felt naked, cold, but I stepped away from the earth and down into the boat, and Charon poled into the dark waters.

Sometimes I caught a glimpse of my hair in Charon's ever-changing, pieced-together body as he navigated the river. But the sight made me feel sick and dizzy, so I looked away, up into the black or down into the water. It was only hair; it would grow back, must grow back, though I didn't know for certain that it would. It had never been cut before.

I remembered Hermes' words about the cost of choice and realized I had made my first payment.

The barge did not glide smoothly. We collided with things that made the creaking boards bump together and jar my feet. The sound was wet, what we hit solid. I saw faces beneath the water, hands reaching out, as if pleading: drowned souls, bodies in the waves. I closed my eyes, rubbed at my skin to warm it.

When we neared land, I scrabbled out of the boat and up onto the rocky bank. Charon, whisperless, turned from me and poled off, back into the blackness and the far end of the shore. I stood trembling, watched him fade away. Once my nerves had calmed, my heart steadied, I turned my head to face fully my destination, the kingdom of the dead.

It stretched, flat, bare earth, as far as my eyes could see. Despite the torches, there was blackness above and all around me, and in the distance loomed a great spindly structure, a gathering of white towers and keeps and tall, wide walkways, lashed together as if with plans drawn from a mad architect's dream. The palace at Olympus was something the mortals had imagined for us, made real with their beliefs. This was a creation no mere mortal could conjure, so chaotic that my eyes ached when they traced its maze of bridges and stairs. The towers were tall, narrow, leaning. Was it all made of marble? It listed and seemed to hunch, like a crippled animal. This broken-down thing must be Hades' home, the palace of the Underworld.

I hesitated, afraid.

Across the dark plain came a quiet avalanche of voices—whispers again, though less distressing than Charon's cobbled-together tongue. I wrapped my arms about myself, chilled to the bone, and forced my legs to move away from the water, toward the white palace and, I hoped, Hades. My skin prickled with goosebumps; a shudder raced up and down my back, as if someone invisible stroked the spokes of my spine. I needed to finish this. I needed to rest. Tense and frightened as I was, listening to dislocated voices, I feared I was in danger of losing my sanity. "Almost there," I spoke softly to myself, and I hurried onward.

The palace was pure white marble, and, as I neared it, I saw the cracks, so many cracks. One of the smaller towers had fallen and crumbled, now a jagged, sad path of broken marble on the ground. I edged around its sharp pieces, crouched to pick up in my hand a cool, soft shard that disintegrated to dust when I squeezed it. Everything here, even the stone, was dying or dead. I felt the dead all around me, felt their eyes watching me, heard their voices speaking of me. But I didn't see any of them, not yet, and I was glad for it. I crawled through a tunnel in the broken tower and found myself before a staircase leading to the doorway of the palace.

If I had assumed Hades would meet me at the entrance, greet me, usher me in with a smile and a bow, I was mistaken. No one was there. I paused at the threshold, uncertain, heart beating faster than a hummingbird's wings.

"Hades?" I called out, cursing myself when my voice shook. I took deep breaths, reminded myself that I had completed my quest, had done what no other god before me had dared to do. I was afraid, but

I was here, free of Zeus, and that was—had to be—enough.

"Hades? Are you here?" I tried again, mustering up the courage to shout. My voice echoed back to me in mockery of a reply: *are you here, are you here, are you here...*

"All right, then," I whispered, and I walked uninvited into the palace of the Underworld.

The hallways twisted and looped around like the tunnels of a rabbit's warren. I thought I was heading in one direction only to find myself veering in a great curve, until I'd made a circle and returned to the beginning again. It was maddening, but I didn't have the strength to be angry. I kept one hand on the marble wall and walked up and down, around and around, hoping that I would find Hades, worried that I would find something horrifying.

When I neared one bend in the corridor, I heard music, and I paused to listen. It was a soft melody from strings, soothing; it drew me forward. I peered around the corner into the open doorway of a large room.

She was dressed in black, all black, and in the fashion of a mortal man. Her feet were bare on the stone-tiled floor, and she'd drawn her hair back into a twist behind her shoulders. She didn't notice me; she was moving in gentle arcs around the room. Dancing, I realized, as I admired her careful gestures and gazed, hypnotized, at the cloud of light she held and whirled and tossed: it separated and coalesced, changing form from a hoop to an orb to a shower of light, flickering over the shadows in the darkened space. And the music—it came from everywhere and nowhere. I felt it in the floor, the walls, inside of myself.

I drew in a quick breath—perhaps I gasped—and then there was silence, and she stood frozen, mid-turn, looking straight into my eyes, lips parted in an expression of surprise. Surprised that I was there, I assumed, spying around corners in the tilting palace of her deep, dark kingdom.

"Hello," I whispered, and I almost laughed, the word sounded so ordinary and out of place. My legs were shaking, but I held her stare and half-smiled. "I've come."

"So you have," Hades replied, straightening. With a flicker of her fingers, the cloud of light winked out. She stood still for a long moment, and then, haltingly—as if uncertain—she held out her arms to me, opened them wide.

It seemed like a dream, all of it—my descent, the horrors of the Styx, Hades' light dance. But my heart was pounding so hard that I heard it as well as felt it, and my tunic was damp and stained, and my hair… I pressed what little remained of it against my neck, shamed suddenly to stand before the goddess of the Underworld in such disarray.

But I could bear it no longer, and I ran across the room to her, buried my face in her shoulder. I did not sob, did not weep, though I wanted to, could feel my lingering strength pool out from the soles of my feet onto the cracked marble floor. I pressed my mouth to her neck, against the dark fabric of her garment, and I breathed her in.

She held me, and it was not a warm embrace, but it was an embrace, nevertheless. When I loosened my grip on her, she backed away, rested her hands on my shoulders at arms' length, and looked me over.

"You chose this," she said simply, and I nodded. She drew me near again, though gingerly, as if she did not know how to comfort but wished to try. My ear pillowed against her breast, I listened to her heartbeat, and its rhythm reminded me of a song I knew.

"Hermes brought you?" she asked, arching back to catch my gaze.

"Yes." And then, because I needed to tell her, needed to explain: "Zeus meant to take me with him to Olympus."

"I see." Shock first, and something akin to anger, stirred the flat pools of her eyes. "Well, he won't have you now."

"No, he won't." I shivered.

"Come with me."

Hades took my hand purposefully and led me down a series of long, dark hallways. I tried to remember our turnings but soon gave up, confused and lost, grateful for Hades' sense of direction. Finally, she stopped before a doorway, and beyond the doorway, there was a small room with a smaller bed and a single oil lamp.

"Sleep," she said, soft and low. "You're safe."

Safe.

I closed my eyes to savor the word and cherished the sensation of Hades' steady presence beside me. "I can scarcely believe I'm here," I whispered. "I'm truly here, inside the earth. With you."

"Sleep now, Persephone," she intoned, as if the words were a spell, and she touched my arm so gently, I felt a tear sting my eye.

"Good night," I whispered, and her skin left

my skin, and I knew without looking that I was golden, golden all over, and then she left, every part of her: her scent, her eyes, her voice like music from another world. I lay down on the bed and stared up at the darkness.

My head and heart were full, but my body was exhausted, and within moments, I fell fast asleep.

Four: Underworld

Persephone, Persephone--where are you?
Oh, my beloved daughter! Zeus, where could she be?
Did you take her? Have you stolen her from me?" My
mother wails and beats her chest and scrabbles for
ash in the fire as the king of the gods laughs and
shrugs and leaves her weeping, alone.

I woke with a start, breathless. My heart felt
as if it would break the cage of my bones. I pressed
my hands against my face, surprised to find my eyes
sore and wet. I'd been crying in my sleep. And my
mother—my mother had cried for me in the dream.
But it was only a dream.

Woozy, I sat up, detangled my legs from the
twisted blankets. I knew where I was, why I was here,
but to wake from a nightmare in this cold place, with
no green in sight, no sunlight, no birdsong… I felt the

weight of the earth pushing down upon me again, and it was only when I lifted my eyes, noticed Hades standing in the doorway, that the weight lifted and I remembered to breathe.

I rose, washed my face, and we walked together; we didn't speak. I had no sense of the time because there was no sky. I supposed, here, time was irrelevant, since nothing grew, nothing changed. The corridors meandered up and down, ending in staircases so narrow that my hips brushed the walls, and I wondered what it all meant, my life, life itself, that it led to such a strange, dark conclusion.

Hades guided me onto a balcony. Instead of stars, my eyes met uninterrupted blackness.

"Your hair," she said, touching the ragged edges that brushed against my ears, one gentle finger grazing against my bare neck.

"I sold it."

We watched the sunless morning in silence. After a little while, I stopped expecting a sunrise.

"I'm sorry," she said. "There are so many...rules in the Underworld. What is received must be in equal value to what is given. These are old laws, older than me—older than the earth." Her hands gripped the marble railing. "I couldn't make it easier for you, though I wanted to."

I reached out and touched her arm. She didn't flinch; she didn't react at all. So I let my hand fall away and whispered, "It was my decision. I rebelled."

"What did you say?" Hades fixed me to the spot with an intensity of gaze I had never seen from her before. I felt pinned, spellbound.

"I rebelled," I repeated doggedly. "Hermes told me—"

"Hermes," she laughed, pressing her fingertips to her temple. "Of course." Her pale face—luminous as a full moon in the dark surrounding us—tightened with agitation. "He is a dear friend but a born meddler. Did he say anything to you about…all of this?"

I hesitated. "All of what? I'm not sure I understand."

Hades chuckled for a moment, nervously, arms folded over her middle.

"This…" She cleared her throat and tried again: "This has never happened before. No one, mortal or immortal, has ever *chosen* to enter the Underworld. We don't know what will come of it."

My heart was sinking. She seemed different from last night, far away, locked up with her thoughts. I felt very alone.

So I remembered Charis' face. I painted it perfectly for my mind's eye, replayed Zeus' unforgivable violation, held the horrid image over my heart like a shield. There were reasons that I had come down to this place, and if I ever forgot them, I would lose myself to despair.

Hades was watching me, but I couldn't read anything from her steady black gaze.

"Persephone, why have you come here, truly?"

"Truly?" I had already told her about Charis, about Zeus and his plan to whisk me up to Olympus. Her question had a deeper motive, I was certain, but I couldn't discern it; she was too distant now. "I came for a chance," I murmured finally, resolve making the words sound sharper than I'd intended. "I came for a choice."

She nodded, expressionless. "Yes, well—you've come a long way. I hope you find what you're seeking." She straightened, shook herself, as if waking from a dream, and then she turned and walked back down the corridor at a brisk pace, beckoning me with a glance over her shoulder. I trotted to catch up. "I was waiting for you to wake so that I could show you the Underworld," she said, and we quickly wound our way through the palace. I took three steps for every one of hers.

"There is so much here that you must learn, see— There is even beauty. It's not much, but it's my home."

I tried to imagine what it must have been like for her, what it continued to be like, her uncountable years underground. Waking to darkness and whispers instead of sunlight and birdsong. Somehow, she seemed contented with the gloom, so I didn't pity her—or myself. Her world was my world now, and I was eager to explore it by her side.

We left the palace and walked together over the hard earth, our footsteps silent beneath the wind of whispered words. I could see, dimly, by the light of the torches, but then something fell over us—like a mist—and I was blind in the thick fog of black. Hades took my hand, squeezed it tightly.

"There are spells of darkness here that descend without warning," she said, her voice low, her breath warm at my ear. "Don't fear them. If you wait a moment, count to ten, they evaporate." And even as she murmured the words, the darkness began to dissolve, break apart like a flock of frightened bats, and I could see again, gaze at the placid planes of Hades' face. A path—darker than the dark earth on which we stood—stretched long and wide before us. I noted the far-off walls of the cavern arching overhead, but my eyes couldn't find the dome, the ceiling, where the walls joined together. When I looked up, I felt a sensation of limitless space, but that couldn't be true: somewhere above us—far, far above us—grass grew. Unless...

Was the Underworld a place you could journey to, physically find, beneath the earth, or was it another world, like Olympus? I had walked here, found the gate. But my mind couldn't make sense of this dark vastness, couldn't connect it in any way to the earth I knew so intimately. Again, I imagined myself caught in a waking dream. Nothing seemed real. Not this path, not Hades' hand in mine, not those stone mounds up ahead, or the sound of water lapping.

But it was the water that coaxed me out of my thoughts. I knew very little, but I knew this place. Hades drew me to stand near to her on the rocky shore of the river Styx. I looked for Charon, listened for him, but we were alone, and I breathed a secret sigh of relief.

"Here the rivers Lethe and Styx mingle together," Hades said, sweeping her arm over the waves. "You've experienced Lethe waters, their healing capabilities. But one drop from these rivers combined, and you would forget all you ever were, all you ever knew." Her eyes held mine, the black of them shining, slick as oil. "Oblivion."

I shivered, chilled.

"But who could ever want oblivion, something so final, so absolute?" I wondered, mystified, even as we were joined by a...being, a soul, I guessed, thin and wispy as smoke from dying embers. He did not acknowledge us—in fact, he walked *through* us—and kneeled down in the water, bent his head to drink.

When he stood, he turned and stared at me with eyes so empty that I took a step backward, broke my hand from Hades' grasp, and moved aside so that he would not pass through me again. He did not appear happier in his oblivion, and a moan escaped his throat, the sound so miserable that I felt my own heart seize in sympathy.

"For all I have seen and all I have done, I would never wish to forget," Hades said, watching the soul shamble, head hanging low on his shoulders, toward the darkness. "But some do. And it is their choice to make."

"Hades…" I began, worrying at my lip with my teeth. "There were—people in the river, drowned in the river, when I came over on the boat…and they reached for me, and their faces were so anguished…"

Hades nodded, her eyes lowered so that the long black lashes shadowed her cheeks.

"Again, an old law—the Underworld is rife with old laws. If you swim into the water, sink into it, the Styx takes you. Keeps you. You can never come out." Hades held both of my hands, positioned herself in front of me, so that her nose tipped toward mine. "Those souls tried to cross back over, to return to the land of the living, but the river trapped them. And they'll be trapped forever."

I swallowed hard; my eyes glazed over as I imagined the horror. What if I had jumped from Charon's boat? To be captured in such a way, wet, cold, dark…and lost for all time—it was worse than any punishment Zeus had ever devised.

"Don't go into the water, Persephone. Promise me."

"I promise." My voiced sounded odd, detached.

Hades pulled me along, and I followed after her, staring at the black waves with a new dread.

We walked in silence until we drew nearer to the mounds of stone. They were not round piles of rock as I had first assumed, but dwellings—smallish, dusty, grey caves, hundreds of them, perhaps thousands, millions. I couldn't make out the end of them; they were lined up like a fastidious child's collection, and they faded into the tunnel of darkness beyond. As we moved among them, wisps fluttered out of the doorways, gathered before us: women, children, men. Here and there dashed the transparent spirits of cats or dogs, and one of the women rode up on a huffing ghost mare. The souls observed Hades and me with blank expressions, and though none of their lips moved, the whispers increased in volume and pitch, a tornado of sound.

Hades inclined her head at the crowd. "Persephone, this is the village of the dead. These souls are mortals whose lives expired. Some have been here for days, some since the beginning of time."

I didn't know what to do, how to act. I gazed at the wispy form of a young girl with hair the color of clouds, and I smiled my warmest smile, but her face closed up tight, and she folded in upon herself, turning away, hunched like a flower too heavy for its stem.

Hades' voice rose to speak over the whispers,

and she addressed the gathering in a fond manner, more like a mother than a queen. "Here is the goddess Persephone," she said, resting her hands on my shoulders, "daughter of Demeter and Zeus. She is my invited guest, and I ask you all to treat her kindly, and welcome her."

Her words were received with awkward stillness, and the whispers buzzed, thick and indecipherable. The souls—so many of them now, and more appearing with every moment—stared at both of us, not with wonderment or even curiosity, but with a mute antipathy. I watched, shocked, as some of the souls sneered at Hades and openly balled their fists.

Still, Hades offered them unruffled words. "Will you not welcome her?" she asked, and it seemed no one would, and I didn't want anyone to; I wanted to go, to never come back. But then a young woman strode forward.

She was more opaque than her companions— almost solid—dressed in a fine white tunic common to the Greeks, hair bound up with dangling, golden tethers. Her eyes flashed, mischievous, and her legs were bare of sandals, and when she stood before me, she cocked her head and grinned.

"A daughter of Zeus, are you?" she proclaimed loudly enough for an echo. I cringed at the reverberation of my father's hated name. But the woman's face held no malice, and her crooked smile softened to one of mild amusement. "Welcome to the Underworld, goddess. We"—she gestured widely— "are the dead."

I was tense, uneasy, surrounded by the gawking souls, and still shaken from my long journey; a nervous giggle escaped my throat. I put a hand to my lips, but the smiling woman laughed now, too.

"I am pleased to meet you," she said in a quieter tone, and she gripped my arm with her strong fingers, like the mortal men do when greeting one another.

"Thank you." I felt a little calmer, though the crowd still stared.

Hades sighed, bowed her head between the two of us, whispered, "They're worse, Pallas. Angrier."

"I do what I can to quell them, but... They've stopped listening to me. They think I'm under your spell..." The woman—Pallas—shook her head and smiled wryly. "They don't trust me, Hades. But, oh, where are my manners? Persephone..." She took my hand, bent over it, kissed it. Her lips lingered for a moment on my fingers, soft but very cold. I shivered involuntarily, and Pallas threw her arms up in the air.

"I've lost my touch with the fairer sex, dear Hades," she laughed. "Tell me, Persephone, is it because I'm—hmm, how do I put this delicately— dead?" She pressed her hands against her hips and winked.

Hades chuckled, and I turned to look at her, surprised. "Persephone, Pallas is my dearest friend in all the Underworld, my faithful companion."

"Oh," I breathed, and my stomach fell. My heart teemed with dreadful feeling: confusion, loneliness, loss. Loss of what? Something I had never had to begin with...

Suddenly, I was furious at myself, and I was blushing. I wanted to hide my face, but there were souls everywhere. And what did it matter? Hades had provided me sanctuary, and I was grateful for it, and I had no rights to expect more, to want more—

"It's not what you think," said Pallas gently, laying her hand on my hot cheek. "Have you never heard my name before, Persephone? Don't you know my tale of woe?" She spoke the last word with a sardonic twist to her lips, but her eyes were dull, saddened.

"I'm not certain—I was very sheltered—"

"Allow me," Hades said, offering Pallas' shoulder a squeeze. "Our lovely Pallas lost her life in a fit of anger and passion, the most potent of mortal, and immortal, emotions."

"Too true," Pallas smiled. "Go on, go on."

"Pallas was the beloved of the goddess Athena. You are familiar with her, Persephone?"

I nodded. "A little, yes."

"They quarreled, and in an...accident of rage, Athena ran Pallas through with a sword."

"Oh, how horrible!" I gasped, agape, but Pallas cocked her head, shrugged her thin shoulders.

"I was mortal, weak, and Athena was strong. We loved..." Her voice broke, but she shrugged again, folded her arms. "We loved hard and deeply, and we fought like wild beasts. She was too wise for me, and I was too impetuous for her.

"It was for a foolish reason that we quarreled—so small, so foolish that, now, I can't remember it. When I died, Hades took pity on me, became a friend to me when I had no one, and no hope." She patted Hades' hand, gazed at her warmly. "And Athena...well, even the gods can't come down to the Underworld for casual visits. I have it on authority, though, that she misses me." Pallas' eyes shone. "She took my name, you know. Pallas Athena." She stared down at her unshod feet. "It has been three hundred years."

My hand found my heart, and it was breaking for her, and I said, "Oh, Pallas," remembering Athena drunk and fondling the mortal girl on Mount Olympus.

"It was a long time ago. But I can't forget it. So Hades takes pity on me. We've become friends, I think."

"Yes, we have," Hades smiled.

I offered my hand to Pallas, and she held it, gazed at it wistfully. "I hope we can be friends, too."

She nodded. "We will. Well, of course we will!" She tucked my wrist in the crook of her arm, grabbed onto Hades with her free hand, and tugged the both of us away from the assembled dead and their strange, sad, whispering village. The sea of souls parted as we passed through, and I was so glad to leave that I smiled widely, caught Hades' eye, and she ducked her head toward me, smiling, too.

I noted again the solidity of Pallas as compared to the wisps of people we left behind. I could not see my hand through her arm, and her footfalls stirred the dust, just like Hades' and mine. I puzzled over it, how alive she seemed, save for the coldness of her skin and a barely there haziness.

"What interests me, Persephone," she said, as we neared the doorway of Hades' palace, "is how you came to the Underworld."

"I walked here," I said simply. She chuckled, patted my hand.

"It's just unusual... No one, except for

Hermes, enters the Underworld unless they've died."

"But why is that?" I asked her. "It was a difficult journey, but not an impossible one, and…" I began to worry that perhaps Zeus would come fetch me, after all, come down here and take me away, punish me, and my mother, and possibly Hades, if he found out where I had gone.

Hades shook her head; her hair gleamed under the torchlight, and her eyes glittered like black stones. "Fear, Persephone. They are immortal, but they fear death more than the mortals fear it. No god or goddess would dare enter my kingdom, because they fear that they could never leave it."

"And could they leave it?" I asked, my mouth dry, palms damp.

"You are free to do as you please."

"I didn't mean— I just wondered—You said that there are laws…"

I was afraid that I had hurt Hades' feelings, or appeared ungrateful, but she gazed past Pallas at me and smiled her gentle smile. "You are free," she said again, "to do as you please. My kingdom is yours, and when you tire of it…your earth will welcome you back."

My heart fluttered like something loose caught in a wind. I wanted to thank Hades, tell her how much I appreciated all she had done for me, how I cherished her kindness, but the proper words wouldn't take shape, and Pallas let go of us both to climb over and through the ruins of the fallen tower. "Truth be told," she said, her back to Hades and me, "the gods are wise to fear this place. There are dangers here, fates worse than death. Have you warned her to keep away from the Styx, Hades?"

"Yes—"

"Everything dark and unseemly lurks hidden in the Underworld. There are horrors unlike any you might find up there, above ground."

"You're frightening her," Hades said, and Pallas glanced at me, her face apologetic. "I don't mean to, but she lives here now, and she needs to know... I would want to know."

"I do want to know," I said, surprised by the strength of my voice, "and I'm not afraid of being afraid."

Pallas turned to me, hooted and clapped her hands. "There it is! That's why you're here, you and no other. It could only be you..." She nodded at Hades, and their eyes locked in a weighted gaze. Pallas' lips curled up into a grin.

We walked through the doorway of the palace.

~*~

I couldn't sleep. Phantom faces of the souls trapped in the river Styx haunted me every time I closed my eyes. Frustrated, I rose and paced my room. Alone with my thoughts, with the dark, I felt crushed down, and my skin was crawling. So I left, well aware that I would never find my way back through the maze of twisting corridors and staircases.

All was so quiet, a deafening quiet that I could not bear, and I almost longed for the chorus of whispers of the dead. The press of silence on my ears was painful.

"Oh! Persephone?"

Pallas—she'd nearly run into me, and she grasped my upper arms to regain her balance.

"I didn't see you. I'm sorry. I thought you were sleeping."

"I couldn't. I hoped a walk might help—"

"Come, come! I've just the thing for restlessness."

I followed her down a corridor that arced to the left, and she pulled me by the hand into an illuminated room—gold-and-white shifting light— occupied by a beautifully carved lyre and Hades.

Pallas dropped to the floor, folded her legs beneath her, took up the lyre and began to strum, the notes clear and bright, sparkling. She grinned as she played, and her joy was contagious.

Hades crossed to me, questions in her eyes, the sphere of light glinting in her palm. I smiled; I was so happy to see her. "I can tell you're busy; I don't mean to interrupt—"

But she smiled, stopped my mouth with her finger, and tossed the orb up over our heads; it showered down upon us, twinkling like tiny stars in the night of her hair.

"How…" I began, and then her hand was in mine, and the light was still falling—no, hovering in the air—and Pallas made the strings sing, bliss to my ears. Hades twirled me around, and I was wrapped in shining gossamer strands, dancing with tendrils of light. I felt wild. Hades' skin glowed, and my heart caught in my throat.

And then she was dancing, too, a whirl of darkness and brilliance.

I moved to the corner, lay my hand against the wall, and watched Hades spin and spin. When the music stopped, she sprawled on the floor beside Pallas, laughing, breathing hard, her black eyes bright.

I felt like a poor child staring through the merchant's window at something beautiful, a treasure, I could never afford.

"Good night," I murmured, so quietly they may not have heard me, and I turned from the room and walked back down the corridor, retracing my sleepless steps. Several wrong turns later, I found my room, and, slowly, I sat down on the bed, stunned.

I knew this feeling. I knew what this was.

I lay down on top of the blankets and closed my eyes to the dark, covered my brow with my hands.

"She's so beautiful," I whispered, and I lay there awake for long hours, wondering.

Five: Pallas

"Wake up, Persephone."

I opened my eyes, rubbed a hand over my face, my hair, unused to its ragged shortness. I blinked to clear my dreams away, and in the dim light of the room, I saw Pallas kneeling beside the bed, smiling at me like someone with a secret. I drew my knees up beneath the blankets and smiled back at her.

"You sleep like the dead," she grinned, and she helped me to my feet. "Hades is in official mode today—she has to greet some new heroes arriving at the Elysian Fields." Pallas faced me, hands on hips, as I bent over the basin to wash my face. "She won't be able to attend to you for awhile, and she *implored* me to look after you. So! Let's see what mischief we can get up to."

I tried to hide my disappointment, but Pallas

made a clucking sound with her tongue and grabbed my hand, leading me out of the room before I could dry off; rivulets of water coursed over my cheeks. "You'll see her soon enough, lovely. Tell me—what do you feel for our queen of the dead?"

"I feel…" I felt so many things for Hades, and it was all so new, I hadn't yet matched words to the feelings. At least, not any words I was prepared to share aloud. "Grateful," I sputtered, "and fond. She's given me my freedom. I don't know how I'll ever repay her for that, but I would like to try."

"Mm," Pallas replied, mysteriously, and she led me with practiced expertise through the meandering maze, holding her tongue all the while. When we stepped out of the palace, my heart sunk just a little: the great dome of blackness arched above, and the flat, dark plane of the Underworld stretched before us. Soon enough, I knew, I would learn to accept the gloom, but my eyes were so hungry for light that they clung to each torch we passed; the weak green glow was never enough.

I listened to the whispers of the Underworld and followed Pallas along the long, hard path beside the river Styx. When we reached the village of the dead, souls watched us but did not speak to us— Pallas moved too determinedly. I caught glimpses of wisp children staring through carved-out windows, of ghostly men and women clustered together, whispering—always whispering. The hairs on the back of my neck rose, and I feared I might lose Pallas in the dull confusion of identical dwellings, so I matched my pace to hers.

"Where are we going?" I finally asked when she paused at the roiling river's edge.

"I want to show you something. Silence, now—I have to concentrate."

To my horror, she knelt down at a place where water lapped stone and thrust her arms shoulder-deep into the river.

"Pallas, no! You can't—"

"Shh."

The water churned, murky and black, and I could see flickers of eyes and limbs beneath the waves. Hands, nail-less and white, snatched at Pallas, but she was calm, resolute. She ignored them completely.

"What are you doing?" I hissed, falling to my knees beside her. She shushed me again and lurched backwards, her arms stretched out over the water. The torchlight revealed a shimmering string clasped in her fists. She held the end of it, and the river hid the rest.

"Pallas—"

"I was in no danger, as long as my face stayed above the water. And now," she smiled at me, her eyes twinkling, "we can cross."

My fingers pulled at the frayed hair against my neck, and I gazed at the string in Pallas' hands. "Have you summoned Charon? With that string?" A panic broke within me at the thought of stepping foot on his barge again, so soon.

"We don't need Charon," Pallas said simply, raising the string over her head, tugging at it, so that the water engulfing its length rippled gently. Planting her feet on the riverbank, she hauled the line; it tautened, glimmering like a silver beam, between her grasp and that of the Styx.

Several moments passed during which nothing else happened; I turned to her, perplexed.

"Wait," she whispered.

So we waited.

Then there was a roar so sudden that I clapped my hands over my ears and cried out. Pallas grinned at me, motioning with her chin. In the distance, the black waters parted, and I saw that the end of the string was tied to a rusted loop on a rotting board—which was attached to the front end of a rotting ship with the river Styx streaming over its edges. As it rose from the depths, the waters closed beneath it, and the craft, at Pallas' urging, drifted quietly to the shore.

"See?" Pallas laughed. "No need for Charon at all!"

"Thank the gods for that," I smiled, relieved and excited.

She leapt onto the ship, jumped up and down to—I guessed—test its soundness. "She's not entirely seaworthy, but she'll do for a short excursion. Come on, Persephone!"

I stepped over the rails, scuffed my sandals on the waterlogged wood. "How do we steer?" I asked, and Pallas pointed her finger at me, then spun about and pointed to the opposite side of the river. I slipped and lost my footing as the ship shuddered and bounced in that direction, away from the village, the palace, Hades.

"You're amazing!" I called to her over the roar of the water, and she shrugged her shoulders, smiling widely, offering me a hand. I held on to her and scrabbled to my feet, wobbling a little with the sway of the boat. I tried not to look too hard at the water, at the doomed souls who reached for us and slapped at the wooden planks.

Finally, the boat nudged against land and

shivered to a halt. We disembarked quickly.

"Why have we come here, Pallas?" I wondered for a moment if she meant to take me back up to the earth—but of course she couldn't go there. The dead weren't permitted to leave the Underworld.

"You'll find out in a moment."

Hoof beats, a hard staccato on the rocky shore.

Before us was the place where gargantuan wall met with the ground, affording a lip of earth a few strides wide before it plunged into the Styx. Along this lip moved two shadows, sleek and black, trotting so effortlessly it seemed they floated—but for the sound of their shoes clipping against rock. I knew them: Hades' chariot horses.

They towered, taller than I remembered. Just out of our reach, they slowed, stopped, snorted, moving against one another and angling their great necks to survey us. Pallas held out one hand, flat, to the largest beast. I watched as he bent his chiseled head to nose her palm, and a red tongue snaked out to lick at her skin.

"Ebon," said Pallas, stroking the neck of this creature with her free hand. "The smaller one is Evening. Together, they pull Hades' chariot."

I stared at them in awe, and Pallas chuckled. "Go on, they don't bite. At least, not often."

She smirked, took my hand and placed it upon Evening's heaving side. He shifted toward me, brushed his great head against my chest and stomach; tears sprung to my eyes. Despite their imposing size and the sense of menace that preceded them, these were earth creatures…alive in the Underworld. They were like me.

"I think Evening is falling in love with you."

"I love horses," I whispered, stroking the dark and tangled mane, brushing the forelock out of his eyes. He and Ebon were mortal through and through, exiles from the world I'd left behind. I wondered how they coped with the sunless gloom of their mistress's realm.

"They're beautiful, aren't they?" asked Pallas. As I nodded my agreement, she added, "Pity that they're blind."

"Oh... Blind." I gazed into Evening's eyes and found a milky whiteness in their depths.

"Blind from birth—the only way they could live here and not go mad." Pallas patted Evening's shoulder. "Horses get along well anywhere if they're blind. They're not like people."

I nodded.

"Persephone, why do you look so sad?"

"I'm not sad... I guess I'm sad for them, trapped here."

"Hades treats them well. Spoils them, to be truthful. And Ebon—" She ruffled the velvet of his nose. "He's getting fat! Hades feeds him too many apples."

When the horses had grown bored of our pampering and wandered off to nose at the ground, looking for grass (which did grow down here, Pallas told me, in a special area Hades had created just for them), I said, "Thank you, Pallas, for bringing me here. I miss the earth—more than I realized."

"I thought you might." She watched me closely. "It's always nice to be reminded of home."

I sat down on the hard ground, felt the chill of it through my tunic. "But isn't this your home now?"

"Isn't it yours?"

I bowed my head. Is it? I wondered. Could it be?

Ebon and Evening moved together as if in an equine dance; they showed no signs of their blindness.

"How is Athena?" Pallas whispered so softly I wondered if I'd even heard her. When I turned in surprise, she was gazing down at me; quickly, she looked away. "Athena?" she murmured, and there was pain in the word…perhaps fear, too.

"I saw her on Olympus," I admitted, grappling with the truth, hoping for the means to conceal it. Again, I saw the Athena of my memory, red-faced and riotous, her arms entangled with another woman's, hands caught up in her hair. I bit my lip, and Pallas sat down beside me.

"I miss her," she said, leaning forward, elbows on her knees. "I dream about her every night. Every night. And when I wake up, sometimes I think I'm still there with her…and then I realize where I am, and I lose her all over again."

"I'm sorry," I whispered.

"It was a long time ago. It seems like yesterday to me. But to her—"

We sat in silence. I watched the churning of the river Styx, and my thoughts drifted along with the dark waters. I thought about my mother. I hoped she wasn't worried for me. I wondered if Zeus knew I was missing.

Most of all, I wondered… Was Hades thinking about me now?

The Elysian Fields—the name was familiar, but I knew nothing about it, told Pallas as much. She crinkled her nose, staring up into the black.

"It's a reward for the heroes. If they've done service in honor of the gods, they can receive a blessing from Zeus, bypass the village of the dead, and live out their eternities in a place of sunshine and golden fields. It's not really so idyllic, though, as much as the heroes talk about it, as much as they dream of going there." She leaned forward and studied her hands. "See, that's all it is—a bright sky and fields of grain, and the heroes sit there for all eternity, alone with their thoughts, trying to forget the men they've killed, the atrocities they've committed, the horrors their eyes have seen. It's…it's worse than the village of the dead. It's a nightmare."

"But Hades welcomes them there?"

"Well…" Pallas sighed. "She speaks with them. She takes away the worst of their pains. Not physical pain—none of the dead feels physical pain in the Underworld, only the ghost of it. But there are other pains, of the mind…and the heart." Her eyelids fluttered for a moment, and she licked her lips. "Many of the heroes came from the wars—they murdered women, children, in the name of Zeus." She shook her head, sneered, and her expression spoke volumes: Pallas hated Zeus, too.

"So Hades helps them," I prompted her, and she nodded.

"She does what she can to ease their transitions. She doesn't have to, but she wants to. She exhausts herself. I've tried to tell her it's a wasted effort. No matter how she counsels them, they all end up the same, sobbing or moping in the field, staring at nothing, lost in the darkness of their own thoughts."

"I'd like to see them."

"You wouldn't. It's depressing beyond

words."

"I'm sure it is, but I would still like to visit, see for myself."

"Perhaps someday Hades will take you there."

I gazed across the Styx.

Besides Pallas, I had had only a handful of interactions with mortals; I knew so little about them. But this is what they had to look forward to, after a long, hard life? Endless darkness, crowded together, waiting for...what?

"That's why they're angry, you know," said Pallas, and if she'd read my mind. I turned to her, and she steepled her fingers, leaned close to me. "That's why I spend so much time in the village. The dead are angry that the heroes have the Elysian Fields and they have only those hollowed-out mounds. I've tried to explain to them that the Elysian Fields are a joke, a cruel trick—but they don't believe me. I'm only one person—and a favorite of Hades, who they distrust. The stories are too strong among them. They won't listen."

A chill crept over my skin, and I shivered, rubbing at my arms. "I'd be angry, too, Pallas."

"Yes, it's terrible. But Hades didn't invent this design. It's all Zeus' doing. How can it be undone? We don't know who created the earth, the Underworld, but the dead end up here by Zeus' decree. I have always wondered—for as long as I've been here—if we were all meant to end up in the Elysian Fields, not just the heroes. And if it were populated, if there were enough souls to form communities, I think it could be a truly beautiful place. But that's beside the point," she shrugged. "The dead blame Hades for everything. They cling stubbornly to the unfairness of it all, and they need a target for their anger."

"But what could they do, other than complain? They're insubstantial… One of them passed straight through me."

"Look at my arm," Pallas said. "See how real it looks. You've felt it; you know it's solid. I'm this way because I believe I should be—because I don't accept the idea that the dead are *less*. Less real, less physical, less important. It's all about belief, Persephone. They think they're nothing, so they look like nothing. Feel like nothing. But if they claimed their own power—" Her eyes were hard, unflinching. "If they banded together, discovered a way to harm Hades… I fear for her."

Pallas' words disturbed me to the core. I felt helpless, and I was so cold, my teeth were chattering. I wanted comfort and would have none, not here.

I took Pallas' proffered hand, and she helped me to my feet.

"Hades thinks I see plots where there are none. But she is too trusting. She loves her people even though they hate her." We began to follow the edge of the river. Unease gnawed at my bones as I watched the waves, unseeing.

The horses noticed our movement and galloped ahead, then hung back, ran ahead again, caught up in a game. Finally, we bid them farewell; they snorted and trotted away, back to their grassy plain, I imagined, black tails streaming behind them like banners snapping in a wind. We watched them go until the darkness swallowed them up.

And then the darkness swallowed us up, too. I was choking on it, suffocating in it, the black was so thick and heavy.

"Persephone!" Pallas called, and I held out my hand, found her frantic fingers.

"Hades told me about these," I said, trying— and failing—to hide the tremor in my voice. "I feel like I've been blindfolded."

"Wait just a moment. There! It's lifting already… See?"

The black cloud evaporated, and I found myself staring at Pallas' infectious smile. She patted my arm. "They're annoying, more than anything. Like a rainstorm. You get used to them."

"I hope I will," I murmured, noting how near we'd wandered to the river in our blinded trek. We could have fallen in, and we might have been dragged under… But we were safe. Safe enough. I inhaled deeply, anxious to return to the palace.

She drew the silver string from the shallows and quickly hauled the boat to the shore.

"How do you do that?" I asked her. "How can you find the string?"

"I can't explain it. Somehow, the string acts like an anchor. And no matter where I dip my hands, I find it, sooner or later."

"Does Charon know about this?" We stepped over the wet, creaking wood. The boat shoved off with a groan, rocking over the waves in the direction of Pallas' extended finger.

"Does it matter?" She grinned at me over her shoulder.

"I don't like him."

"That's all right. He doesn't like anyone."

I tilted my chin upward, closed my eyes, hummed a little to myself to block out the whispers of the underwater dead.

When we reached the other side of the bank, Pallas and I hopped off the boat, and it sunk deep into the waters without a sound.

"Well, that was an adventure, wasn't it?"

"It was," I agreed, but my thoughts were elsewhere. We climbed the embankment, and when the village of the dead came into sight, I began to drag my feet.

"Must we go through it? Isn't there another way?"

"Take courage, goddess Persephone," Pallas teased me. Still, she held my hand, tucked it through her arm. "The Underworld is a funny place—if you wish to go somewhere, there are certain roads you must travel, or you will never arrive at your desired destination. It's alive, in that way. It has a mind of its own."

"Tell me about the places here. I want to know more, all there is to know."

Arm in arm, we began to stroll toward the rows of cave dwellings, and now we had to raise our voices to speak above the whispering.

"Well," she cocked her head, "there is the village of the dead, of course. The river Styx. The Elysian Fields—which no one can find without Hades' guidance. She herself is the key. If she wills it, the fields simply appear.

"There are tunnels branching off from the caves along that far wall," she continued, gesturing. "Don't go exploring. They hide abominations—the gods' creations, most of them—monsters that would eat you as soon as look at you. And," she sighed, voice lowering, "there's also the entrance to

Tartarus."

"Tartarus?"

She exhaled heavily. "I don't like to speak the word. It's the deepest, foulest place in all the earth. Ghastly, through and through."

"And none of these creatures ever come out? Out here?"

She swallowed and kept her eyes on the path. "No, not usually."

The dead surrounded us, but I tried not to notice, or listen. Instead, I stared at the dwellings—what did they remind me of? I had encountered something like them before, and as we walked among them, I remembered: burial mounds. Old, old creations of the truly ancient peoples, dug up and formed with rock, dirt and prayers. They were sacred, those mounds, and these mounds resembled them, but there was no sense of sanctity, only despair.

A child sat on the ground, making circles with his finger in the dust. He waved a dirty hand as we passed. I waved back, smiled faintly, but Pallas shook her head, pushed me forward.

We had almost come to the start of the village—I could see the path to Hades' palace just ahead—when a gathering of wisps confronted us, held out their arms as if to block us, and I glanced at Pallas, who had stopped in deference to them. I supposed we could move through them—they were like vapors, barely there—but I waited by Pallas' side, shivering.

"Hageus," she addressed the tallest ghost, a wide-shouldered, fierce-eyed woman.

"You spent last night in the palace. Preferential treatment, eh? What's next? Will you get a place in the fields?"

Pallas and Hageus stared at one another with schooled expressions, but their eyes flashed dangerously.

"Don't be a fool," Pallas scoffed. "If I had the choice—and I did—I'd choose the village over the fields. You've not seen the fields, my friend. I told you; they're insufferable: endless rows of grain, merciless sun and nothing else but silence. And regret."

"But you've *seen* them." Hageus strode forward, her amorphous eyes lit with a strange light. She touched Pallas' shoulders, and I was struck by how transparent Hageus truly was in comparison to Pallas. She rolled like fog.

"She's seen them! I told you—she's seen them!"

The other souls gathered close, pressing in on all sides. I had assumed that I would be able to move through them, but when I pressed back, I came up against a resistant wall of flesh. They were solid to the touch, and strong.

"Calm yourselves." Pallas' words cut into the rising fervor like a knife. "I saw the fields for just a moment, a long time ago. You forget—Athena wanted me kept there."

"Because you have always been the gods' favorite!" Hageus cried out, and shouts rose up, growls of assent. Someone grabbed at my hair, and I stumbled back, collided with a dead woman who hissed in my ear.

"The gods would give you anything if you asked for it!"

"But not my life." Pallas' words were lost in a

cacophony of screams. Hageus ripped Pallas' tunic, and I cried out, crushed between the angry souls until I could no longer draw a breath, until I grew so weak, I began to sink down—

"Enough."

They dispersed like smoke, and swathed in the mist stood Hades. Her black eyes were narrowed, the brows drawn sharp.

"Listen to me," she whispered, deathly quiet. The wisps faced her, all at once, as if compelled by a force beyond their control. "Never again," said Hades, pronouncing the words like a spell, a curse. She stepped before me, took my hand. "Do not touch her ever again."

Pallas nodded almost imperceptibly at Hades, exchanged a short, meaningful look with her, before turning back toward the village—toward her own dwelling, perhaps. There were no sounds, not a whisper, as Hades led me away from the gaping crowd.

I had never felt so tired, and I had to trot to keep pace with Hades' long strides.

She didn't speak a word, didn't address me at all, not until we'd passed through the doorway of the palace, and then she stopped and turned to me, gathered me into her arms, pulled my head to her chest.

I lost myself in the rhythm of her heartbeat, willed my own to pound in time to hers.

"Are you all right?" she whispered.

"Yes. Thank you for—"

"Don't thank me." She pulled away, rubbed at her eyes. "Forgive me," she sighed, and, after a heartbeat more, Hades turned and strode down

---

the corridor. My eyes lost her to the darkness.

I slumped against the wall, too exhausted to stand proud and straight, like any well-bred goddess should. What would my mother think of me now, dusty, humbled, shorn? I hunched over my heart, felt its drumming—imagined I heard a name in its irregular tempo.

Had there been true danger? I was immortal, but Hades had been so angry at the crush of souls and, just now, so mournful.

I wasn't wounded, but I felt drained of energy, too tired to ponder any more questions. Too tired, really, to search for my room, but I wandered the palace, anyway, stumbling, lost, and the instant I gave up hope, there it was, my long, low bed. I didn't know what time it was, if time existed here, but I had to rest, and when I fell upon the pallet, only one thought flared before sleep overtook my mind: Hades had thought of me.

Six: Elysian

It was impossible to tell if it was morning or the zenith of the night. I tossed and turned, slept in snatches, woke again and again in a panic—compressed by the earth, the dark. At last, I got up, smoothed my short, tousled hair as best as I could, and went wandering through the corridors of the palace. There was nothing else to do.

I found Hades' throne room. I had walked past it before but never lingered. Here rows of glowing torches lined the walls, and a great black chair stood at the center, larger than necessary, rough and square. I traced my fingers over the dark marble, felt the carvings on the armrests: shrouded people stood in a row, lifting their arms to Hades, who knelt, embracing a weeping child.

A door behind the throne led to a shadowed

chamber. I heard a stirring within and wandered closer, stood, hesitant, in the doorway, blinking at the darkness.

"Persephone?"

Hades.

She had told me, when we encountered each other in the Immortals Forest, that she didn't believe in coincidences. Again and again, night after night, I found her without looking for her; I wondered if it was by chance.

She reclined on a low bed similar to my own, but—like everything else in the space—it was black as night. Blacker, for the absence of stars. Scrolls littered the floor, and she held one open in her hands, but she dropped it, rose hastily, gave me a bemused smile.

"I'm so sorry to bother you," I murmured, "*again*." But she'd already crossed the room to me, reached for my hand. I gave it to her, as I had done so many times before, but now a hot current raced through me; it flashed like lightning.

"Bad dreams?" she asked, and cleared her throat. She offered me a seat on her pallet, but I shook my head, sinking to the floor, careful not to tear the scrolls.

"No. Just restlessness. I haven't eaten in days, I realize now."

"Oh?" She tilted her head, sat down on the bed. "I didn't realize you needed food."

"I don't, not really. But I've always eaten, anyway. It's habit more than requirement. I do miss fruit," I smiled, thinking of the pomegranate I'd hidden in my room. I couldn't bear to eat it, my one reminder of home. "I doubt you have much of that down here, though."

She shrugged, smiling now, too.

She was so beautiful when she smiled.

"No, not at the moment. I gather apples for the horses whenever I surface in your forest, but they've eaten them all—greedy beasts that they are. Now they're subsisting on the grasses and grains that I grow for them. To be honest, we have little food of any sort here in the Underworld."

I leaned back on my hands, gazed at the tapestry hanging on the wall adjacent to the door. It depicted a large tree with widespread roots and glorious, sky-scraping branches. I studied it, transfixed.

Hades observed my interest. "A young weaver made that for me…a very long time ago. It's one of the few offerings I've ever been honored with. Most mortals are less than fond of me, for obvious reasons." She laughed, smiling faintly. "It's called the tree of life. See how the roots and branches spiral together? The cycle of life and death, never-ending. Eternity."

"It's beautiful," I managed, though I saw in the weaving the lines of my favorite oak; Charis and I had spent countless afternoons in its boughs, wrapped up in one another's arms, feeling never-ending ourselves. I hadn't known the ache of her loss in days—I'd been too preoccupied with hiding, escaping my predestined path. Now the sorrow struck me hard, and I tore my eyes from the tree, stared down at my hands.

"Have I upset you?" Hades inquired quietly.

"No. I was only remembering someone." A strange thought occurred to me, and I wondered why I hadn't considered it before. "If…if someone were dead," I began, "would you know it? Would she— they be here?"

Hades inclined her head, pinning me with her fathomless eyes. "I know the name and history of every person, every creature, who has lived and died. No sparrow falls without my knowledge, and acknowledgment, of it."

I pondered this, awed by the woman seated before me, her solemn strength. Summoning up my courage, I leaned forward and strung together the words in my mind.

"Do you remember…" I paused, started again: "I told you a story. I told you how I loved someone very much. How I lost her. Her name was Charis."

"Yes. I remember."

"Zeus—he transformed her." My voice was barely a whisper, and I dared not look into Hades' eyes. "I don't know what that means, if she still lives, in the form of a plant, if her spirit is trapped or if…" I swallowed. "Could you tell me if Charis, the nymph, is here in your Underworld?"

I glanced up at her now, and her face was still, placid—the mask again. She sat for a moment, unmoving, and then rose to stand at the purposeless window; there was nothing but black beyond it. She clasped her hands behind her back.

"She is not here, Persephone." Her tone was flat, and it matched my feelings.

I didn't know how to react. Should I be relieved that Charis was yet alive? Should I grieve that her soul was bound in the roots of a rose? Would it have been better if she'd simply died? What did she feel, malformed into something unmoving, unfeeling, inhuman? What did she think about, who did she talk to, with only the soil and the stars for companions?

I wrapped my arms around my knees, reflected in the silence. Hades turned to face me; her onyx eyes were worried, and her concern unraveled something within my chest.

"Thank you," I whispered.

"You're welcome," she whispered back.

~*~

Had I been here for a week? A year? Time passed strangely in the Underworld, where the days were unmeasured, the nights indiscernible. Pallas took me again to visit Evening and Ebon, but for the most part, I remained indoors, wandering the passages, learning to navigate them with some accuracy.

Hades was a sometime, somber companion. She spoke so sparingly. When we passed one another in the halls, I nodded, and she nodded, and I felt her absence with a pang in my heart. And when my wanderings led me to her chamber—by chance, fate, or, more often, by my own design—we didn't converse much, but I was soothed by her company. Her dark eyes enclosed depths I was eager to explore, and when they rested on me, a flush crept along my arms, my neck, and I felt warm, even while seated on the cold marble floor.

I was lost, directionless, in an Underworld dream. All was calm, quiet, dark.

"Where do you go at night?" Pallas whispered one day, brushing out my hair with a blue sapphire comb. Precious gems were as common as rocks here.

There was little light to be caught by the comb's facets, but squares of silver still danced over the black walls as Pallas dragged the thick teeth through my hair, which was growing back quickly, long enough now to glance my shoulders.

"Nowhere in particular." I winced when she tore through a tangle. "Ouch!" Another tangle.

She chuckled. "Everywhere is nowhere in particular in the Underworld." Next to my ear, breath hot, she whispered, "Even Hades is nowhere here."

I felt numb, for the most part. Perhaps my heart, too, was turning to stone. I'd heard legends about Hades' heart: a black diamond some claimed it was. Cold and hard. But I knew it was neither. She intoned the names of the newly dead each day like a prayer, her eyes soft with compassion. And each day, she gazed at me, and…I knew I was seen.

The stories whispered about her were lies, born of misunderstanding, ignorance and fear. She had deep love for the mortals she presided over, every one of them, even those, like Hageus, who scorned her openly. I couldn't understand it, why she cared so much about these fragile, often disdainful beings. What did they have to do with the gods?

I dared to question her about it once, and her response surprised me.

"Have you ever observed a mortal family?"

I shook my head.

"They're like…" She smiled. "They're like the branches of a tree in your forest, bound together by a shared origin, and that bond is very hard to break. They rarely take life for granted, as the immortals do, because they can't—it's a limited gift. Inevitably, they will die, and they know this, know it every moment, with every breath. But the knowing is the true gift, because they cherish time all the more, hold onto it as tightly as they can, hold each other tighter still.

"Families reunite in my kingdom, years, sometimes decades after their earthly parting, and the affection they express, the tears of true joy— There's no match for that beauty in all the wonders of Olympus.

"It's love," she said, smiling gently at me. "Unconditional. And forever."

"Perhaps, but love isn't a talent reserved for mortals. Gods love, too, deeply—I...I know this to be true."

Her smile faded. For a moment I feared she wouldn't speak again, she looked so withdrawn.

"Hades?"

Her eyes found mine, shone at me, intense. "I believe you. I believe you have loved sincerely. But I have never met any other god, or goddess, who knew the true meaning of love, or valued it as the precious thing that it is. And I don't mean to appear pessimistic, but I have lived for a very long time, Persephone." She lowered her chin, looked down at her hands. "So long."

I stared at her, and she lifted her gaze, stared at me, and—it made no sense, given the somber topic of conversation—but I felt as if my heart had finally flung open its doors, to her, to the mortals, to everything below and above the earth. I felt full up of love, and I feared my feelings would overflow. I feared I would speak too fondly, or presume too much. I searched for safe words.

"What of Pallas?" I heard myself whisper,

because I ached every time she mentioned Athena's name. "She's alone here, always will be. Athena is immortal and— I saw her on Olympus, Hades. She was…she held—"

"You know as well as I do that Athena has forgotten Pallas. There is no offense in loving again when one's love is lost. But I have spoken with Athena, offered to arrange a meeting between Pallas and herself—it is forbidden, but I could do it, would do it." Hades scowled bitterly. "She refused, claimed Pallas exaggerated, that they had never been more than casual lovers. Perhaps, for Athena, that was true."

"You haven't told Pallas any of this?"

"No, it's not my story to tell. Still, I think she knows, no matter how she wishes it otherwise."

"My heart breaks for her," I said, unsurprised by Hades' admission about Athena. And I couldn't deny that most of the gods in my acquaintance were fickle creatures—and often cruel. But not Hades. Never Hades. "She is lucky to have you, such a loyal friend."

"I am lucky to have her," she smiled, her eyes flicking over my face. "And you."

My heart stilled.

Quickly, she changed course. "Do you know why they call me the Hospitable One?"

I inhaled, reeling with unspent emotion, and shook my head.

"It's because my realm will always have room for more. Sometimes they call me the Rich One. And…" she smirked, "less flattering things. The mortals fear my name, will not speak it. They've built me no temples. Everyone cowers before the lord of the dead—who is, as you can see, no lord at all."

I managed a weak smile. "No, indeed."

"They fear a god who doesn't even exist, but it doesn't truly matter what I am; they fear me all the same."

"Why? Why can't they see…"

"I represent the end, and that terrifies them."

They are fools, then, I wanted to say. *Who could ever fear so lovely a soul as you? Who could fail to love you, once they knew how good, how noble, how beautiful you are, more worthy of worship than all of the gods combined?*

But I was no longer thinking of the mortals.

I bowed my head, held my tongue.

~*~

One night, I woke screaming. I dreamed I was being buried alive. I craved light and wide-open spaces so desperately, I couldn't bear their lack even in the oblivion of sleep.

Hades appeared by my bedside within moments, offered me her arms, held me as I sobbed softly on her shoulder. And when I calmed down, she told me stories—stories of her people, her ghosts, their lives and their loves. Her steady heartbeat against my ear was companionable, familiar now.

I fell asleep with my head pillowed on her breast, and—for the first time since my arrival in the Underworld—I rested peacefully.

She was not there when I woke. My hand found the depression of her body on my pallet. Still warm. She had stayed with me, reclined beside me.

I slid into the empty space she'd left behind.

~*~

As much I longed for Hades' company, she had duties, so many duties. Wars raged on the earth, and there were battalions of deaths each day, and heroes, designated by Zeus, eager to gain entrance to the Elysian Fields. Hades listened to their tales, encouraged them to release their painful memories. Sometimes she administered waters from the river Lethe. Sometimes she used meditative magics. She told me these things, and I tried to imagine what the experience was like for her. It cost her so much; she could never truly rest. Sometimes she fell asleep in the middle of speaking to me, waking when her head fell, with a start and an apology.

"Come with me," she said, finally, when we stumbled upon each other in the palace entryway. She was about to leave again. "You should know, see this for yourself."

Eagerly I took her hand and followed her outside, but we paused together on the last step of the staircase.

"How..." she breathed, staring.

The fallen tower—the broken tower that we'd had to climb over, through, countless times—was gone. No remnant, not a pebble, of it remained.

"Hades?" I moved my hand to her arm.

We both turned and gazed at the palace behind us. There, where there had been a large gap in the marble—a hole where the broken tower once stood—we beheld an impossible sight. The tower was repaired, restored, as if it had never crumbled.

"Oh," Hades said, and our wide eyes locked,

and we both laughed, perplexed. But soon enough, she resumed her pace, walking easily over the cleared path, slowly, thoughtfully. I followed behind.

"It's believed that the kingdoms of Poseidon, Zeus, and myself are linked to us, physically, to our souls, our emotions. When Poseidon rages, the waves arc higher than mountains. When Zeus is provoked, the sky explodes with lightning. If the Underworld truly is connected to me, perhaps that's why it's changing...rearranging."

"But how could it change?" I asked her. "It's stone, and stone can't grow, can't reform itself. It's not alive."

"No. But *I* am," she whispered.

I puzzled over this. The tower was connected to Hades, and it had been broken, irreparably so. Now it was one piece again, as good as new. Perhaps better than new. The metaphor was obvious, and it pained my heart even as it warmed it. The palace, with its disjointed design, its maze of passageways, its loose, softened stone—did it reflect Hades' inner shape? Did she truly feel so lost, so ruined?

We passed through the village of the dead without incident, skirted along the shining bank of the River Styx, and then we broke away, found the middle of a dark plain, and there Hades stopped, regarded the dark above her, head cocked as if she were listening to something I could not hear.

"What is it?" I whispered, heart quickening, but she shook her head, closed her eyes. Had a monster escaped from its cave? One of the monsters Pallas had warned me about? Was it stalking us now? I determined not to be afraid, but my traitorous hands were shaking. Just as my mother's hands had shaken when—

"Persephone." Hades covered my hands with her own, and I felt still, comforted. "It's all right. There's nothing to fear. There's nothing here, save for the door."

"What door?"

She looked into my eyes, bent her neck so that her forehead nearly grazed my own. I could feel her breath travel the contours of my face, and she was so close, our mouths could touch, would touch if I just—

The great darkness of the Underworld dissolved around us.

There was light! So much light that I had to shield my eyes. I felt my skin soak it up, sun-starved, and I twirled in a circle, my head tilted backward, my whole body trembling, reveling in this burst of summer, this golden warmth.

We were surrounded by wheat, waist-deep in it—glorious, sweet-smelling grains that stood tall and shimmering in the hot sunshine. There was nothing but wheat, fields of it, hazy and blurred along the edges of the horizon.

Pain stilled my heart when I passed my hand over the dry, papery leaves, the tall stalks. I swept my fingers across them as if they were lyre strings, instruments of music.

My mother grew the grasses, fruit, trees and flowers, but she loved the grains best. Her people worshipped her for the grains she provided them, for their yearly harvest, for their breads. I remembered how she and I used to chase each other through the whispering wheat. It bent for us as we moved through it, flattened itself to the ground, bowing.

I missed her profoundly, but I refused to feel

sorry for myself. She was up there somewhere, living her life, seeding the earth, fulfilling her purpose, her passion. And I was down here, awash with light, Hades—pale skin shining like moonstone beneath this false sun—warm by my side.

She took my hand, held it like her dearest jewel.

"The Elysian Fields," she whispered, head bent low, her mouth near my ear. "Listen."

I listened. The grain slithered together, shushing with the same soft sound my mother had made to me when I was a baby, lying in my cradle woven of reeds. It was the sound of comfort for me, of home, and I closed my eyes to hear it without distractions. My body began to sway, back and forth, in time with the slowly sifting grain.

It was sublime.

"Keep listening," Hades' gentle voice urged me. "More deeply—fall into the sound."

I held my eyes shut, loosened my grip on Hades' hand, and listened hard, probing beyond the susurrations.

"Where am I?"

It was a boy's voice, urgent, bewildered.

I raised my lashes. Before us, in a small circle of earth nestled among the grains, crouched a youth. He could not have been more than fifteen mortal years old—lithe, muscled, wrapped in scraps of leather and bent, misshapen metals. White scars gleamed like chalk on his skin, and he kept one eye clamped closed, because, I assumed, it was injured, or gone.

"Where am I?" he entreated again, looking up at Hades. "Do you know? Did you bring me here?"

Hades let go of my hand and knelt down beside him, placed her palms on his hunched shoulders.

"You are home," Hades said, in a tone both soft and firm. "A victor, a hero, come back from the wars. We are all so proud of you. Your father is so proud of you."

The youth shook his head. His brows furrowed together, and tears streaked down his face, dripped from his chin to the soft turned soil beneath him. "I'm not a hero. I was afraid."

"You are a hero," Hades insisted in the same steady voice, gentle, certain. "They sing songs of your conquests. They tell the tale of your victory when they sit around the cooking fires."

"I killed her," the boy spoke through his sobs, rocking back and forth, his eyes glazed over. "She was on her knees in the mud. She begged me to spare her, but I had to…I had my orders—"

"You're home now," Hades whispered again, even as he began to wail. He fell forward, pressed his face into the earth, his whole body quaking with the intensity of his grief. Hades gazed up at me for a moment, her eyes brimming with sadness. I wanted to comfort her, even as she strove so single-mindedly to soothe the war-torn young man, crying now like a child lost in the dark woods.

Hades wrapped her arms around his shoulders, and he sat up, buried his wet face in her breast.

She sighed a deep, silent sigh.

How did she cope with this? Every day, for years…centuries, longer?

I swiped the back of my hand across my face, realized I was crying, too.

The wheat swayed, back and forth, forth and back, hypnotic, and as I stared at it, relaxed my eyes upon its calm waves of gold, the field changed, grew more focused. There were broken patches of wheat now, and scattered over the ground, as far as I could see, were men and women, young and old. Many sobbed, some stared, forlorn, up at the sky, some paced, some wreaked violence—tearing at their clothing, at their hair, at the monotony of wheat.

The shushing of the fields was drowned in moans and howls, and I knew, then, why Pallas hated this place. I hated it, too. The irony of it. Beauty and light mocking the unsightliness of mortal suffering. The sun shone too brightly, blithe and indifferent, and I sunk to my knees at Hades' side.

These people, their pain—it was too much. Deep within me, I felt my heart crack.

The youth was quiet now, curled up like a kitten on the wheat-littered earth, his good eye gazing blankly at the apathetic blue sky. Hades turned to me, grimacing.

"Do you want to stay, Persephone?" she asked. "Would you like to see more?"

I felt shamed for my initial euphoria at sight of the gleaming field of wheat, blind to the horrors that it concealed, as blind as this sky.

"No, please," I whispered.

Hades gazed at me with such gentleness. Again, she leaned in close, so that the tips of our noses met, and the tears clinging to my lashes dampened her face.

I bowed my head lower, and even behind my closed eyelids, I saw the darkness descend, felt the cold of it surround me, extinguishing the hot forged sun.

It was all gone—the fields; the broken, mislaid souls.

I squinted in the black landscape, reached out my hands. Hades took them, held them, pressed them against her chest.

"It's all right," she murmured to me, and I whispered, "no," because it was so unfair—she spent her immortal lifetime comforting others, and now she had to comfort me, too. When would she be comforted? When would she be permitted to rest?

But I was weak; I couldn't stop my tears.

"Perhaps I was wrong to take you there. But you asked me so many questions about it, and I felt you had to see it with your own eyes to understand."

"Yes," I said, my voice unfamiliar, rough, "I had to see it. Thank you, Hades. Pallas tried to tell me, but... I had to see it. The villagers are mad to long for that place. To blame you for depriving them of it."

She shook her head, inhaled deeply, avoiding my gaze.

I bit my lip. There were so many things I wished to say to her. I wanted to tell her how I admired her. How brave she was, how selfless.

I wanted to tell her how beautiful she looked here, now, even as the corners of her mouth dipped downward, her eyes lowered so that I noticed the delicate pink skin below her brows. "You do that," I whispered. "You go there every day. You speak with them, but they don't remember your visits. They don't listen. They don't change. So why... Why do you put yourself through this trauma, in vain?"

"I must." She regarded me evenly. "If I can

provide peace for even one moment, one moment in an eternity of moments, my efforts, none of them, were in vain."

"You're mercy itself," I smiled, shaking my head. "How different the world would be if you, not Zeus, had drawn the longest straw."

Her mouth opened—whether from surprise, offense, or disagreement, I could not tell—but she offered no reply, and I didn't expect one from her. We sat down together on the dusty black rock, our backs to the distant Styx.

I wondered… How many people—heroes—inhabited the Elysian Fields? What had they done to earn that professed honor? What violence had they inflicted in the name of Zeus?

I thought of my father, the abominations he committed, commanded, condoned, and I seethed with disgust for him, and shook with pity for his misguided followers.

Hades leaned against me, shoulder to shoulder, and I welcomed her weight, her warmth.

"You are too good," I said, "and he—" I could not bring myself to pronounce his name again; my mouth felt sour with the taste of it. "He belongs in Tartarus with the monsters."

She stared at me sadly. "Persephone…"

"Why must any of this happen? Why must these places exist, the Underworld, the Elysian Fields? I don't understand, Hades. It…none of it makes any sense."

"Perhaps it isn't meant to."

I shook my head. "He tricked you. He banished you here to secure his own playground. Why have you let him do this to you?"

She stood abruptly, brushed clinging bits of wheat from her dark clothing. "Someday I'll tell you the story." She offered me her hand and a gentle smile. "But not today."

We walked back to the palace slowly, and I was so consumed with my thoughts that I scarcely noticed when we passed through the village of the dead. The people seemed subdued, though, disinterested in our presence, and I was grateful for it.

Hades parted from me in the corridor that led to my room, and I found Pallas lounging upon my pallet.

"What happened?" she asked me, rising to her feet. "Your face—Have you been crying?"

I crossed my arms, collapsed on top of the blankets. "I'm all right," I sighed. "Only a little tired."

"Oh, Persephone. She took you there, didn't she? You saw the heroes—"

"Yes."

She reached out as if to offer me comfort, but I was heart-sore, raw, and did not want to be touched. I ran my fingers through my hair, tugging at the tangles, and when I felt salt tears sting my eyes, I turned toward the pillow, hiding my face.

"What's wrong, Persephone?"

The question jarred me.

What *was* wrong?

Was it the brutality those heroes had meted out in Zeus' honor, or their endless suffering? Was it Zeus' cruelty, or was it my own self-pity?

Was it the fact that, some nights, I dreamed of my beloved Charis, but, more often, I dreamed of Hades…and hated myself for it? Why did I dream of

Hades? It was too cruel. I had loved completely, and I had lost terribly, and I knew better than to love again.

And Hades—Hades was protective of me, gentle with me, but she was gentle with the dead in the village, protective of them even though they despised her.

"I'll leave you, then," Pallas said, and I could hear the hurt in her voice. I wanted to call out to her, but she left too quickly, and I closed my eyes, squeezed out the last of my tears, as my thoughts looped around and around, twisted into knotted circles.

I fell asleep.

I dreamed of a river filled with souls caught like flotsam by the current. A boat poled across the river's expanse, navigated by a fluid, patchwork creature who stared at me with a single blue eye. He held out a hand, but when I reached to take it, he drew back so that I lost my balance, fell into the water, dragged away and down deep by the desperate, hopeless dead.

I opened my eyes, rose, and pressed my hot face against the cool marble of the wall.

I had to see Hades.

I found her in her chamber, stretched out on her side upon the bed. Her long hair was unbound; it lay like silk over her pillow. Her black eyes caught me, held me where I stood.

The silence yawned between us, but it crackled, alive.

"You're resting," I whispered. "I'll go—"

"No. Tell me." She beckoned with her hand for me to sit down beside her.

I crossed the space between us and seated

myself slowly, on edge, self-conscious.

Whenever I sat next to Pallas and our knees bumped together, I hardly noticed. When she touched my shoulder, embraced me, brushed my hair, I felt nothing but comfort, the easy rapport of friendship.

But now, as I sat so near to Hades, I was aware of every sensation; my body tensed, as if in expectation, and it was more than I could bear. She drew up her legs, curled them beneath her, and positioned herself even closer to me, peering at my face. The black curtain of her hair gleamed beneath the torchlight.

I looked at her, swallowed, my mouth dry as papyrus. I didn't know what to say. I was warm, too warm. I felt like a traitor to Charis, to myself.

"Everything is so complicated," I said, finally, because the silence was suffocating me, and because I wanted to hear her voice.

"Sometimes I think we imagine things to be more complicated than are."

She leaned against me. When her arm snaked around my shoulders, I pillowed my head upon her heart.

Seven: Charon

"It's easy, Persephone," Pallas said. "Just put your hands into the water, feel around for a bit until you grasp the string, and pull." She finished lacing up her sandals, stood and stretched her arms over her head.

Hades would be busy with her duties all day long, and Pallas was determined to speak to the villagers again. Her crusade to convince them that Hades was not their enemy, that the Elysian Fields was a place of horror, not hope, was not going well. The anger and bitterness that permeated the village of the dead was palpable now, and there was a sense of bated breath, as if something were about to happen—but it never did.

Rather than spending another day alone, Pallas suggested I pass my time with Ebon and Evening, but I had never summoned the boat before, and my nerves jangled at the thought of dipping my fingers into the roiling Styx.

But I was lonely, and I couldn't endure any more hours wandering the palace, tormented by my thoughts.

When I arrived at the riverbank, I sat down on the stone and stared hard into the murky water. I couldn't see it, the string, though Pallas had sworn to me, again and again, that it was there, was always there, no matter where or when she searched for it.

I watched the river, my eyes mesmerized by the rippling black sheen of it, until a face surfaced with the rise of a wave. Sallow eyes ogled me, and then, crazed, a pair of white, pitted arms splashed upward, hands clutching at the air.

I scrambled from the edge and swallowed hard.

The soul fought the river's flow but soon enough gave up, drifted off, far beyond my sight. These waters teemed with the dead, I knew, and I pitied them their fate. But I was one misstep, one slip-up, one moment of inattention away from sharing that fate, and the knowledge froze my feet in place.

Still...

The Underworld was my home now. I couldn't depend upon Hades and Pallas forever.

I set my jaw. It would be easy, just like Pallas said. So easy that I'd laugh at myself afterward, mock my own cowardice.

And I missed the horses, the sweet, lovely earthiness of them.

Resolute, I crouched down on the ground, crawled up to the edge of the water—close, but not too close.

I couldn't see anything, or anyone, lurking under the waves.

Do it. Do it now.

I plunged my right hand into the dark shallows, and my fingers quested madly for the string.

It wasn't there—I couldn't find it… What if the boat obeyed only Pallas? What if it wasn't there for me, couldn't be there, because it was hers alone? Like Hades and the Elysian Fields…

I was so focused that I didn't notice him until he was nearly upon me. Panicked, I thrust myself upright so quickly that I lost my balance, fell onto my knees in the water. The cold of it rippled through me as I scrambled, undignified and panting, away from the river and onto the bank.

Charon stood at the front of his boat, pole stuck in the river bottom. The blue eye of my nightmares was lost in a maelstrom of bones and flesh, churning.

"What were you doing, Persephone?" he asked, and the words repeated in a child's voice, an old man's voice, a shrieking girl's voice—echoing.

"I was going to swim across," I lied.

"That would have been unwise."

I stared at him. I wanted to look away, needed to, but I refused to show him any of my weaknesses.

"I will take you across if you ask me to, Persephone."

Goosebumps broke out over my arms.

I should say no.

I should go back to the palace, sit down on my bed and wait, wait hours and hours, for Hades to return.

I had done it before. And it was safe there. I

would be as safe as a bird in a cage, and just as lonely.

My skin prickled. I thought, *Well—I won't take his hand. It will be all right as long as I don't touch him. And then I'll be free. I'll run with the horses...*

I couldn't think about it. I simply had to act.

I stepped into his boat, and he said nothing, though a squeal of laughter uncoiled from somewhere within him. The floor rocked beneath my feet as I moved to the farthest edge of the barge, opposite Charon, and he began to pole across the great expanse of black waters.

I stared ahead, watched for the appearance of the riverbank on the other side of the Underworld. Charon startled me when he whistled, strung together a high-pitched, discordant melody, and voices—male and female—sang along in thin voices. I couldn't make out any of the words, but it seemed a sad song.

"How are you getting along at the palace, Persephone?"

The question came from nowhere and everywhere, a chorus of it, repeating again and again, as if spoken by ten different people. I glared at Charon, at the roiling pieces of mortals' bodies that floated within his shape.

"Very well," I murmured.

"That is good to hear, good to hear." It was a young woman's voice this time, sultry and slippery as silk. "I've heard that things are...unstable now in the Underworld." The whisper slithered over my arms, and I shook it off, sighed deeply, but he was no longer looking at me, instead staring at the departing shore.

"What have you heard?" I asked him. "What do you know?"

"I know what I know, and I know what you know," he answered, and continued poling, whistling a tune that reminded me of a child's lullaby. "I know that the dead are unhappy. But they should be unhappy. They're dead." Laughter threaded the air like filament; I felt it, a ticklish spider's web, clinging to my face.

"It is hard to feel happy in a place devoid of light, rife with death...isn't it, Persephone? Have you ever lost someone to death? There's never an end to death. It goes on and on and on and on..."

I craned my neck, searching for the riverbank, willing it to appear. I wouldn't speak to him, encourage him. I had made a mistake, boarding this boat, and I ached to feel earth beneath my feet again.

"The dead are angry," he hissed. I recoiled at the harshness of his words, leaning back slightly over the water. "They want equality, release and relief, and they will never find those things under the rule of Hades."

My hands clenched at my sides, but I refused to take Charon's bait. The boat tilted dangerously; I clung to the sides of it while he laughed.

"Be careful, Persephone." It sounded like a warning, and he repeated it over and over in a chilling, singsong voice.

I dug my nails into my hands deeper and deeper as we rolled along, trying my best to ignore the ferryman and his nonsensical ramblings, multiplied, amplified, by a hundred different voices.

Dark thoughts agitated me further: He could push me overboard at any moment. He could tip the boat sideways, shake it until I let go.

I couldn't help it—I cried out when the shore appeared, a dark, wet swath of emerald gleaming under the torches' glow.

The boat collided with the riverbank, and I flew out of it as if my sandals were winged. Charon did not grab for me, as I feared he would, but he did not turn to go, either, and his blue eye stared.

"Please leave," I said.

He began to whistle again; the sound shivered through my bones.

"Farewell, Persephone," he whispered above a cacophony of terrible, mocking laughter. "Be careful. Be very careful."

I had to watch him maneuver the boat around, pole through the dark waters until he vanished, finally, consumed by the blessed blackness. I stood and stared for a little while longer, to assure myself that he was truly gone, that he wouldn't turn and come back.

I felt filthy, tainted; I wanted to scrub my skin clean.

When my heartbeat steadied, I inhaled deeply several times and then followed the edge of the riverbank, chirruping for the horses.

I heard their hooves, distant at first, then nearing. I clasped my hands in front of me, waited, and then Ebon and Evening appeared, shaking their black manes. I laughed at the sight of them, buried my nose in their shoulders, breathed deeply their good, earthy smells. They whinnied at me, and the sound, after Charon's mad music, was like a balm.

I needed this. I needed the wildness of them. When I was with them, I remembered things I'd almost forgotten—clover, honey, clouds.

I scrubbed their backs with my fingers, and I petted their soft noses, and I chased them up and down the riverbank until my chest ached from the exertion.

I lost track of time. Had it been hours or minutes? Lying on my side on the stone, watching the horses frolic together, I began to feel tired, but I couldn't sleep here. And I couldn't cross the river. I would never ask Charon to ferry me back. My skin hived at the mere thought of him. Besides, he might ask for payment again, and I had nothing at all to give him.

The horses came to me, as if they sensed my anxiety, and they nosed me with their beautiful, gleaming heads.

I would have to wait. Sooner or later, Hades would realize I was missing, and Pallas would tell her where I'd gone. Exhausted, both of them, after a trying day, they would rescue me from my foolishness. And I would feel like a bothersome child and hide away in my room.

I didn't want Hades to think of me as a child.

I bit my lip and traced my hand over Ebon's silky muzzle.

What if I could find the silver string, after all? Maybe I hadn't done it properly the first time. Maybe I'd given up too soon, distracted by Charon's uninvited presence.

It would be cowardly not to try.

I stood up on the bank, gazed down at the opaque waters, and I felt very small and limited. The dark waves crested; the wretched souls wailed. To me, these people were indistinguishable, a mass of waterlogged faces, swollen, grasping hands. But they had lived once, loved once. I wondered about their stories. I wondered who missed them now.

The river raged before me as if furious at its own fate, a wet, dark pit of sorrow. I stared down at it, into it, spellbound.

This time, when I dunked my arms into the water, I was calmer, more patient. I bent my back so that my elbows were submerged, and I felt around, grabbing at pebbles. Pallas said the water could not harm me as long as my face stayed above it. It seemed a strange law, but so many things were strange here, and I had to believe it was true—for the sake of my peace of mind.

But this wasn't working. There was no string. Not here, not in the shallows.

So I waded into the water. I'd seen Pallas wade in once, when she'd been frustrated and unable to find the string right away. I had gaped in terror as the river licked at her thighs, but, almost instantly, a silver strand floated to the surface, leapt like a fish into her hands.

I didn't know what else to do; it was my last hope for saving myself.

The water engulfed my hips, no string appeared, and my soul screamed that I must turn back. I was so afraid that, for a moment, I forgot how to walk, how to coordinate my movements. My teeth clacked together from the cold, and there were things—long, loathsome things—brushing up against my legs. Were they snakes, limbs?

I swept my hands around beneath the water, searching for the string, and took another lurching step.

There was a drop-off, and I lost my balance. I floundered, kicking up great arcs of water, but my head sunk down, into darkness. With a moan, I surfaced, gulping a mouthful of the fetid liquid. I swallowed it, spit, bobbed gracelessly, kicked with my legs, thrust outward with my arms, but I was confused, and too cold, and I'd wandered too deeply. Devoured by fear, hair plastered to my face, I realized with horror what had just happened: I'd plunged underwater, completely underwater. What did that mean—was I trapped now, forever? Was I stuck in the Styx, with the river souls?

A rush of water rocked me backward, and I was submerged again, and I struggled but couldn't rise, couldn't open my eyes, and now I felt hands, hands, hands—soft-skinned, plucking hands—grabbing at my legs and arms, pressing down on my head, holding me under. I thrashed, screamed, choked on water, lashed out with all of my immortal strength against the groping horrors surrounding me.

Gods can't drown. But this was the river Styx, and I wondered if customary rules applied to it. Within moments, the dark water swallowed me. I sunk down and down, arms stretched over my head, making useless motions.

I missed my mother.

I wanted Hades.

I drifted, weightless.

There was a tug and a push. More souls, I guessed, nudging at my yielding body. But then I heard a scream, and it wasn't human, and I came back into myself, found the will to fight again, and I thrust my hips hard, like a sea nymph swimming, and my hands entangled in something fibrous—it felt like hair.

I heard the scream again, but it wasn't a scream, no. It was a neigh.

I wrapped the hair around my wrists, and I soared to the surface. My mouth gulped at the air, and I coughed until I felt my chest split in two. My eyes were bleary; I tried to rub at them, but my hands were too caught up in his mane—Ebon's mane. Only his eyes, his nose were visible above the water, and, below, his powerful hooves churned. I clutched at his neck as he pulled me along.

On the shore, we both staggered out of the shallows. My legs gave way beneath me, and Ebon dragged me further inland, since my hands were still entangled in his hair. Finally, I fell free, my shoulder blades jarring against the stone.

Ebon stood quivering, snorting, huffing water through his nose, eyes rolled back, tossing his massive head back and forth, over and over. Evening, out of sight on the other side of the river, tore the air with his scream, frightened for his companion.

I couldn't breathe properly, so I coughed on my hands and knees until I had spat out the black water, and I spit until it was all gone, though a slime coated my mouth, my tongue. I closed my eyes and pressed my forehead to the earth and breathed in and out, deep, ragged inhalations, while I tried to understand how it was possible—why I had been permitted to escape the river Styx.

A gentle nose nudged my stomach, once, twice, and I gazed up at the dark, dripping creature. "Thank you," I whispered, reached up my hand. He placed his nose beneath my fingers and rooted upward as I stroked him. Turning, then, he waded down into the deeper waters and began the long, treacherous swim back to Evening.

I watched him go, shaking, in shock. Could I have died? Really, truly died? Or would I have simply been trapped, lost in a sea of corpses forever, and never again see Hades, lose myself in her infinite eyes... A fate so much worse than death.

But I had been spared. I was soaked and stunned, but I was well, whole, thanks to Ebon.

It was a slow, fretful walk to Hades' palace. I was too fatigued to hurry, but I had to get back before Pallas, before Hades, had to wash and make myself presentable. I didn't want them to know how foolish I'd been, how recklessly I'd behaved. I didn't want Hades to know I'd broken my promise to her to stay away from the Styx.

I seethed at myself as I stalked up the palace steps, ran through the now-familiar maze of passageways. Why had I been so proud? Why had I risked my life just to prove a point—or, if was honest, to avoid disappointing my only friends? They were kind and genuine. If their opinions about me changed for the worse at finding me boatless, helpless, I would have deserved that judgment, and I should have accepted it with grace.

And what, exactly, did I think Hades' opinion of me was, anyway? More foolishness, to dare hope that the goddess of the dead, the woman who had offered me sanctuary, a home, out of simple, instinctive compassion, could ever—

She stood before me in the shadowed hallway. Her lips parted and her dark eyes widened at sight of my drowned appearance.

I was so taken aback, so humiliated, that I

stood mutely, shivering, staring at her like a dumbstruck animal caught in a trap.

I didn't know what she was thinking, never knew what she was thinking.

"I just...I had an accident, but..."

I didn't have the strength to invent a lie, and I didn't want to tell her the truth—though she could probably guess at it, at least in part, just by looking at me. In that moment, I felt so ashamed, and I was so tired, so weak, that, overwhelmed, I tried to slip past her.

"Persephone." She lay a hand on my arm, and her eyes swept down the length of me, from my matted wet hair to my soggy sandals, and back up again.

I swallowed the lump in my throat, lowered my gaze, but she coaxed my chin up with the tips of her fingers. Her black eyes shone; her beauty struck me like a blow.

"Persephone," she whispered again, and there was so much warmth in that pronouncement. I cherished the sound, even as I hunched my shoulders and bit my lip.

I couldn't cope with this, couldn't even stand, so I slid down, back against the wall, and sat with my arms wrapped around my knocking knees.

Wordlessly, Hades eased herself down beside me. The heat of her body made my shivers intensify; I wanted to bury myself in it. I leaned, hesitant, against her shoulder, just barely touching her with my damp skin. She made no protest, moved nearer to me, and my heavy head slumped down against the side of her neck.

I heard her heartbeat—or was it mine? It beat

fast and loud.

Hades didn't ask me why my clothes were wet, why my hair smelled of foul water and death. She didn't ask about the bruises on my arms, or why there were tears in the skin of my wrists. She didn't ask why I was so cold, why I was shaking, or even, when I began to cry, why I was upset.

We sat in silence, and after I had wept noiselessly for a little while, she drew up onto her knees and pulled me to her, embracing me fully with both of her arms. I didn't worry about my wet garments; I didn't care that I looked like the risen dead. None of that mattered—nothing mattered—except for this moment. This moment. I nestled it in the soft center of my heart.

We sat against the wall like that until—exhausted, comforted—I drifted into a light sleep. I woke when she lifted me up, gazed at her in wonderment as she carried me through the passageways, over the threshold of my room, and settled me down on the bed. She covered me with blankets, drew them up to my chin, and smoothed back the damp hair that was clinging to my face.

And then she sat near my feet, staring at her hands and the floor.

When I jerked awake from a terror of black waters and grasping hands, the sour taste of death in my mouth, she was there at once; she pressed the length of her body against my back, encircled me with her arms again, steadied me while I trembled.

But I trembled from the nearness of her, and I ached over the distance that I so desperately wished to close.

"Shh, Persephone. You're safe," she

whispered.

My heart tumbled over with gratitude. I was safe, alive, and I determined to never take a second of my immortal life for granted again.

Eight: Cerberus

P allas collapsed on her pallet,
arms crooked loosely behind her head. "It's a lost
cause. They're fools; they won't listen."

"They didn't listen yesterday. They didn't
listen the day before that. They never listen, but still
you cling to hope." I seated myself on the floor,
rested my elbows on the bed. "What's changed
today?"

Her eyes were dark, and her mood was
solemn, and she made no reply. She was like this
often: she spent too much time in the village of the
dead, offering up disregarded arguments, shouting
over the slurs flung at her by the band of dissenters.

Ever since my near drowning in the Styx,
Charon's words had haunted me, and I felt nothing
but despair when I thought of the dead, their misery,

and their hatred for Hades.

I patted Pallas' shoulder awkwardly, sighed. "Hades will return soon. You should speak with her—"

"I *can't* talk to her about this. She mustn't know how bad things truly are. You don't understand." Pallas buried her face in her hands. It was a long moment before she looked up, strain and stress evident in her red-rimmed eyes. I offered my arms to her, and she scooted near, jutted her chin against my shoulder. I felt it there, a distinct weight, but I gazed, worried, at the top of her head; I could see through it now, through all of her body, as easily as I could see through the village's dead.

"She has a right to know…" But my words sounded unconvinced, even to me. If we told Hades about the riots, the rising undercurrent of hostility, she would spend hours and energy she didn't have to spare attempting to appease the dead. Even an immortal could be pushed to the limit, driven mad. We lived forever, but we were not invincible, not omnipotent. We could be depleted, lessened… We could wither.

I couldn't bear the thought of Hades sacrificing herself for the sake of these ignorant souls. It enraged me, how immensely wrong their assumptions were about their lone, devoted protector.

"Why are they so unswayable?" I wondered aloud. "Doesn't it seem…odd to you? Where did these notions come from, and why have they rooted so deeply?"

"I wish I knew."

"Let me help you. Perhaps together we could—"

"Thank you, I appreciate the thought, but..."
She rubbed at her eyes, looked at me glumly, sighed.
"Persephone, you don't realize how much Hades—"

We both turned toward the doorway at the
sound of sandals scuffing on stone.

Hades pushed the shadows aside as she
paused in the space just outside my room. She smiled
at Pallas, who sat up straighter on the bed and bowed
her chin low.

"How are you, Pallas, Persephone?"

"I'm well, " I said, casting furtive glances in
Pallas' direction. She stared back at me, shook her
head meaningfully. I nodded.

"Forgive me for leaving so suddenly, Hades,
but I must rest." Pallas patted the top of my head
gently, and when she stood, she offered Hades a hasty
embrace. "Enjoy your evening."

"Thank you," Hades called to her, as she
hurried from the room, her bare feet slapping against
the marble floor.

"Is Pallas all right?" she asked me, and I
hesitated.

"I—I don't know. I'm worried about her
appearance. She's...fading."

"I've noticed that." Hades moved into the
room and crouched down beside me. "I'll track her
down later, ask her what the matter is. But right
now..." She smiled at me, black eyes bright. "I went
somewhere today."

I gazed at her questioningly, and she took my
hand. "Come, let me show you. I brought you
something back. A gift."

Mystified, I rose and crossed the room with
her, followed as she led me through unfamiliar,

downward spiraling corridors. We descended a staircase, lined with flickering torches, that felt never-ending; it stretched far below the surface of the earth, deep within the belly of the palace.

As my feet carried me down the last flight of steps, I stared in awe at the rocky formations of a massive cavern; stones shaped like dripping fangs hung from the arched roof and poked up here and there from the damp ground.

"What is this place, Hades? And what gift can you have hidden so deeply?"

She shook her head and smiled a smile full of secrets. We moved to the center of the space—Hades insisted that I hold her arm; the rock beneath our feet was slick—and then she did something unexpected: she fell to her knees, whistled, offered her hands to the darkness.

"Come," she said, and I heard a distant whine, high-pitched, excited.

I lowered myself beside her, stared into the darkness.

"Come," she called again, and presently it came: a small creature slinking away from the cave's shadows.

It was a small dog, a puppy, scarcely old enough to be separated from its mother, but it seemed sturdy, confident. At sight of Hades, it scurried over the stone, sliding, and thrust its little paws into her lap. She ruffled its fur, grinning.

It was an adorable scene, and Hades' joy was infectious, but I couldn't help noting the obvious: the puppy had four legs, one tail, and three heads.

"What…is it?" I asked, as the dog cocked its ears—all six of them—at me, crept to my side and sniffed my knees. Hades shooed it closer, and it crawled into my lap, pressed paws against my chest, and licked my face with surprising care and concentration, first with one tongue, then the second and the third. Three smooth puppy tongues bathed my cheeks and chin, and I laughed out loud—it tickled too much. Hades laughed, too, and the cavern echoed with the sounds of our mirth.

"This is Cerberus," said Hades, petting the central head. It rolled back on its thick neck and licked her fingers. "Do you like him?"

"He's monstrous," I grinned. "And, no, I love him." I pressed my nose against his warm little shoulder; it was so comforting, the familiar animal scent. I'd played with wolves in the Immortals Forest and sometimes napped with them, my head resting upon a pillow of thick grey fur, cozy and safe in their den.

"Well, then," Hades smiled gently, "he's yours."

I gazed down at the squirming ball of fluff and heads in my lap, the most precious, most beautiful gift I could ever imagine—and then I looked at Hades. She was watching me shyly, her eyes dark and soft.

"How can I thank you?" I breathed, and Hades' lips parted; I stared at them, my heart like thunder, and I made my second choice.

I nudged Cerberus off of my lap, leaned forward, one palm flat on the ground, the other, trembling, snaked around Hades' neck, and I kissed her.

She was yielding, and she smelled like the earth, my earth, and I pressed harder against her mouth, because I could never be close enough; but I felt her lips slacken, and I immediately drew back, breathing hard, worried that I had gone too far, offended her, ruined…everything.

I cursed her dark eyes, the impenetrable blackness of them, gazing at me so steadily.

"Forgive me—"

"No," she whispered, "forgive me, Persephone, for waiting so long to do this."

A lick of fire burned through me when her lips found mine, and I felt too hungry, too eager, but she felt it, too—she must have—because the kiss deepened, blossomed, lush.

I had wanted this…I had wanted her from the moment we met on Mount Olympus. Some part of me always knew, and it had laid in wait, counting down the days, hours, minutes, until finally...*now*.

Cerberus chose that inopportune moment to bat at our arms with his clumsy paws.

Hades broke away, laughed a little, shaking her head in mock annoyance at the unremorseful creature.

I stared at the goddess of the Underworld, speechless, spellbound, flushed—until Cerberus pawed at my arm again, and I couldn't help it—I laughed, too. We smiled at each other and pet his sweet trio of heads, and we sat, knee to knee, cradled by tussocks of hardened earth. Cerberus crawled between us and began to slug around a tinkling shard of crystal with paws that were already large and would, someday, be monstrously huge. Along with the rest of him.

"Where did he come from?" My voice was hoarse with emotion. Hades touched my knee, traced secret patterns over the fabric of my tunic. It was a familiar, fond touch, and it made me shiver.

"Echidna," Hades said then, and I shook my head, uncomprehending.

She smiled at me, leaned against an outcropping of stone. "Echidna is a monster; she nests beneath the Underworld. She has many monstrous children, and she suckles them there. For Zeus." Hades caught my eye and sighed, with a small shrug of her shoulders. "Monsters for the gods' amusement, monsters to pit heroes against, so they can prove their mettle. Divine entertainment." She tickled the puppy beneath one of his chins. "But Cerberus was always intended for me—promised, before he was born."

"He seems...well, just like any other puppy. He looks like a miniature monster, but he's as sweet as a lamb." Cerberus licked my hand furiously, tail wagging, while I spoke about him.

"I hope you can keep him that way. He was only just born... He hasn't suckled Echidna's poisonous milk. I made certain of it."

"Thank you, Hades." I didn't know what else to say.

He was a priceless gift, and I loved him dearly. I petted his three heads, gazed down into his sleepy, puppy eyes and felt a deep, abiding warmth spread out from my heart to envelop him. He wiggled and rolled onto his back and pillowed one of his heads on my leg.

"I promised to tell you my story," said Hades then, so quietly. "Would you like to hear it now?"

I stared, perplexed, at Hades, the taste of her still lingering on my lips, and she stared back at me, at my eyes, my mouth.

"Yes, please tell me." I reached out for her hand, and she gave it to me, smiling warmly, and stroked her thumb over my skin.

"I don't know where to begin."

I inhaled and squeezed her hand; her voice was trembling.

"Zeus and I were 'brother' and 'sister'—as much as divinely created beings, embodiments of power, can be brother and sister. We heralded together, with Poseidon, the start of a new era. We were our mother's shining children."

"You have a mother," I breathed, stunned. I couldn't imagine a time without the three elder gods; I had assumed that they had simply always been.

"In a sense. We were…created." Hades' eyes roamed the shallow crevices of the cave's walls. "We were made for spite's sake, but—our mother loved us. I should explain…

"Before the world was made, there was darkness and dark land, and, above, the beautiful heavens." She held out her free hand, palm up, and above it, a golden light began to glow. "The dark land was called Gaea, the mother of all things. She had existed always, and she would always exist. She loved the sky—Uranus—with a holy love, and together they created the earth.

"First, she had six sons and six daughters. These were the Titans, and they were beautiful creatures. Uranus and Gaea adored them. But Gaea had more children and more children, each one uglier than the one before, and Uranus was jealous that Gaea lavished her love on such hideous things. So he took his hated children and cast them into the deepest, darkest pit inside of Gaea—Tartarus."

Silent, amazed, I watched as the light quivering over Hades' hand separated, dimmed, reformed into spheres of darkness.

"Gaea was angry at Uranus for this betrayal, and she made a dagger of the hardest metals from her heart. She gave it to her firstborn children, the beautiful ones, and begged them to slay their father. But the Titans were afraid and hid themselves away—save one, the bravest, Cronus. He obeyed Gaea's wish, took up the dagger and brutally attacked Uranus.

"Uranus was crippled and disgraced by his son, and he went...away.

"Gaea took Pontus, the ocean, as her new lover, and she asked Cronus to free his brothers and sisters from the pit of Tartarus. But Cronus was drunk on the power of defeating his father, and he refused."

The spheres of darkness inflated, revealed silhouettes of tormented faces, weeping silently. I ducked my head, heart beating too fast. The history I had thought I'd known was untrue. There was a beginning before the beginning, and it was rooted in cruelty.

"Cronus loved a woman—a beautiful, beautiful woman." Hades' eyes gleamed, and I watched a tear slip from her eye. "Her name was Rhea. She was my mother." She let go of my hand with a soft squeeze and crossed her arms over her chest; the spheres vanished.

"Cronus knew that his children would be even more powerful than he, and so history would repeat itself—son defeating father." Hades' face hardened now, the planes of her cheeks rigid. "Rhea gave birth to five children, and Cronus devoured each of them whole."

She paused for a moment, and I slid beside her, lay my hand upon her leg. I puzzled the pieces of her story together in my head and hoped I was mistaken.

"You…you were one of the five? You were devoured by Cronus?"

She nodded.

"We spent a hundred years in his belly, Poseidon and Hestia and Hera and me, and your own mother, Persephone. Demeter was there, too."

I gasped. "How…how is that possible?" I pressed a hand over my heart, as if to stop up the pain. It had to be true; Hades said it was true. But how had I never known? My mother…

Cerberus was sprawled against my legs, licking my feet, and now I swept him up into my arms, held him close. But he struggled from my grasp and resettled on my lap, grunted, snuffled with his nose, and closed his eyes, instantly asleep.

"We don't remember much from that time," Hades continued. "When Rhea produced her sixth child, she knew she had to stop the cycle, do something to protect the baby… She didn't want this child to suffer. So she begged Gaea to hide him away, and Gaea agreed.

"That baby was Zeus, and he grew up wild, safe and free, under Gaea's protection.

"As always, Gaea had a plan. She raised Zeus herself, trained him to be powerful beyond measure—powerful enough to strike down his father. Cronus was tricked, became sick, and he had no choice but to remove us from his belly. We emerged fully grown and strong, and when we found Zeus, we joined him in declaring war upon the Titans. Together, the six of us—we were unstoppable."

Hades bit her lip, gazed at me with an apologetic smile. "Do you want to hear more, Persephone? It's a harsh tale, and…" She traced her fingers over my cheek, over my neck, awakening a new surge of passion within me. "I could finish it another time."

But this story was important, to her and to me, and I urged her to go on. "I want to know, Hades. I want to know everything about you."

For a long moment, she watched me, her eyes flicking over my face, her lips curving softly. Finally, she nodded and stared out at the darkness surrounding us. "We released Gaea's ugly sons and daughters from the pit of Tartarus. Gaea was so pleased with us. The Titans didn't stand a chance. It was the bloodiest battle, the most vicious…" Her voice trailed off, and she was silent for several thudding heartbeats. "Darkness incarnate. That's what it was."

She looked up. "But it was over, the Titans had lost, and in glory and undefeated, Zeus banished them to Tartarus. Gaea…she was so angry. She tried to get Zeus to reconsider—with violence. She created the most fearsome monsters she could imagine, Typhon and his mate, Echidna, to destroy Zeus. But they were defeated, too, and Gaea… Gaea gave up." Hades shifted, sighed, and Cerberus woke for a moment, sneezed, fell off of my lap, and then was asleep again.

"In the end, we gathered, victorious. But it was an empty victory. We all knew it, all of us but Zeus. He was mad with power.

"We divided the kingdoms of the world

---

amongst us, and that's when I saw him truly, knew him for what he was."

"You all fought together," I whispered. "You defeated the Titans together. It wasn't Zeus alone. You were equals, all of you. Why haven't you fought back?" I couldn't help myself. The injustice sparked a fire of rage within me. Zeus—how I hated him in that moment, with all that I was, with all that I ever was. My hate burned and ached and clawed and ravaged. For once, just once, I wanted him to suffer, as everyone who ever knew him suffered. I wanted to inflict him pain, wanted to erase that gloating smile from his mouth forever.

I shook, my hands clenched into fists, until Hades touched me, gently, gently, her fingers grazing my bared shoulder. I shuddered, crawled toward her, melted into her, my face pressed against her chest.

"Why did you let him do this to you?" I whispered. "How could you let him hurt you so much, Hades? You were powerful—you *are* powerful."

She traced looping patterns upon the palms of my hand.

"I don't know," she said quietly. "It never mattered to me, what happened to me. I didn't…care. And I'm close to Gaea—despite all that happened, she adopted me, became a sort of mother to me, when Rhea was banished away. She…she's become something more now. She's different, changing. I can't blame her for the horrors that happened so long ago. As much as I've hated Zeus—and I've hated him, Persephone—I've learned to forgive him, too. Gaea has forgiven him. Nothing stays the same forever. Nothing can."

I leaned toward her, and she nuzzled against my ear, her breath warm. "There will come a time when I am no longer needed in this place. It has been foretold. I've bided my time, waiting."

Hades pressed her lips against my neck, kissed me. "And you, Persephone... You were foretold, too. I never wanted anything—" her mouth moved softly, gently over my skin "—until I wanted you."

I sat up and looked upon her face, her plain, dear, beautiful face, with her long, straight nose and her solemn eyes. I found perfection in every feature, though it was her heart I loved best.

When she drew her hand through my hair and gently pressed her mouth to mine, I drank her in like nectar, deep and deeper until all was red and ruby, and her skin, her hands, her mouth burned me up. I was an ember, bright, flame and fire, burning from the exquisite scorch of finger, tongue.

I was made over, made beautiful beneath her touch, and my soul cried out for her, to her, fiercely. I broke away, breathing hard, and the goddess of the dead gazed at me as if I were the loveliest creature she had ever seen, and hers, hers alone.

For the first time, I could read her fathomless eyes. I saw love there, and I touched her, had to touch her. I gathered her face in my hands, whispered a silent prayer of gratitude to the stars, to myself, as I kissed her lips.

The memory of Charis rose within me, and though there was still pain, deep pain, I discovered something else: peace. I had loved and lost, and now... Love had found me again, brought me back to life in the land of the dead.

"What are you thinking?" Hades asked when

we drew apart, when I stared into her eyes and knew—knew all I'd ever need to know.

"Nothing," I said truthfully. "Just feeling."

Cerberus had wandered away, and we watched him now lift his leg against the cave wall. "Unmannered beast," Hades laughed, and he galloped into her arms. "We should take him up to the palace…"

"Oh, all those stairs!" I sighed, returning her smile. My heart felt so light, unguarded. I realized, with a start, that I was happy. It had been so long since I was happy.

We stood and—hands clasped—urged Cerberus to follow us up the steps. Perhaps it was his monster blood, or just his puppy nature, but he raced ahead of us, paws padding, claws clicking. Soon, he was out of sight beyond the spiral.

We walked slowly—pausing every few steps to kiss—and when we finally mounted the ground floor of the palace, I found the nearest bench and collapsed upon it to catch my breath. Cerberus was sitting primly, wagging his tail, as his heads picked fights with each other. It was absurd and hilarious, and we sat together and laughed.

Pallas found us there, holding hands, arms interlaced, my lips lingering on Hades' neck.

She stared, her brows peaked, and she grinned so hard that her eyes crinkled at the corners. "Finally! It's about time."

Then she knelt down to play with the puppy.

Nine: Gaea

Sometimes, Hades slept beside me.
We kissed one another good night, nothing more, but
the warmth of our bodies sang a heated lullaby that
calmed me to an easy sleep. I nestled my head upon
her shoulder, breathed in the secretive scent of her, of
moss, deep caverns. My nights were finally peaceful,
and my dreams were all of her.

I dreamed I stood in bright, sunlit fields, grass
licking at my ankles, Hades' mouth hot against mine.
In waking life, I suppressed my deeper urges; I sensed
that both of us needed for things to unfold slowly.
And, to be honest, I was afraid; my head was crowded
with so many disruptive thoughts, climbing one atop
the other—though it took only one brush of her lips to
drive them all away, to bind me fast to here, now.

I felt an insatiable need to be near her, to
never waste a moment. At times, I was so blissful that

I believed my heart would leap from my chest; but when I was alone, I had strange thoughts, and I worried about the dead, and Zeus, and their dark intentions. My command over my fate seemed tenuous, vulnerable.

Still, I was falling in love, and I savored it; Hades intoxicated me, her kisses like the sweetest spell.

I remembered her story, every word of it, and—one day—when she'd returned from the fields, I asked her a question I'd been wondering about. "Gaea..." I began, stroking Cerberus in my lap. "You said she's like a mother to you. Do you visit her?"

She raised her brows and frowned, slightly, kneeling down beside me on the throne room floor, her hand alternately petting each of Cerberus' three heads. "Yes. Why do you wish to know?"

"May I see her?"

She sat back on her heels, quiet, thinking. She looked so young, so soft, that I reached out for her, held my hand against her cheek.

Slowly, tracing her fingers over the curve of my arm, she nodded. "I'll take you to her. Now, if you'd like."

I had never seen the entrance to the pit of Tartarus, had never ventured near enough to its black maw for a glimpse. Pallas' descriptions of it had terrified me—of the sharp-toothed monsters that lived within. Monsters, monsters, she said, over and over, until my mind conjured up appalling images, and my soul ordered me to stay away.

As we approached the entrance now, I trembled from head to toe, gripping Hades' arm so tightly that I must have cut off the flow of her blood.

She chuckled at me, as if I were a child afraid of shadows, and prised my fingers gently.

"Persephone," she murmured, placing a kiss upon my brow. "Nothing will harm you in my kingdom, not when you're with me."

"Truly?"

"I promise you."

But we weren't going to enter Tartarus, I realized with immeasurable relief; Gaea's chambers lay to the right of that fearsome black pit: it was just a small break in the rocks, easy to miss. We had to slide sideways and duck our heads to pass through it, and I saw, just barely, that we stood in a long, narrow cave. I followed Hades, grasping the cool hand she stretched back for me. There were no torches here, so she was my eyes, and we moved together slowly, quietly. My mind wandered, and it was easy to imagine that we were the only people left, two small warm creatures in a sunless world.

Hades paused, and I pressed my face against her back. "What is it?" I breathed, heart racing, thinking of beasts with hungry mouths. She turned to me, found my lips, and calmed my nerves with a kiss.

"Listen," she breathed, drawing back, her breath warm on my face.

I heard nothing but the thunder of my pulse. But, then, above that rhythm, I began to pick out another: a deeper sound, thumping low, like blood, like drums.

It came upon us gradually, beating down the passageway, cadenced, until it found us at last and was everywhere, pounding around us, into us, until the music was one with me, and I felt I had to dance or die, and my heart was too full; it couldn't contain this beauty, this sweet, swollen rhythm, a holy beat.

And then it faded away, and silence took its place.

"No," I whispered, but Hades held my hand, led me further down, deeper into the earth.

"It'll come again," she told me, wrapping her arm about my waist to guide me around a sudden bend.

"But what was it? It was so beautiful!"

"It was the voice of the earth, singing praises of Gaea. A hymn for her."

"Hymn?"

"A devotion," she said. "Something sung in honor, wonder, out of the purest love."

As we walked, the path beneath our feet sloping always downward, down, down, down— deeper than I had known possible—the rhythm, the hymn, rose and fell. Sometimes it seemed the walls were singing, vibrating, alive and primal.

I tripped over a rock—what I assumed to be a rock; it was far too dark to know for certain. I fell against Hades, and she caught me, her hands cool on my elbows. "Wait, Persephone. I'm sorry. I've grown too used to the darkness. I should have done this before."

I inhaled a quick breath as a light came between us, illuminating Hades' solemn face. It was a golden sphere, hovering over her palms, twinkling in the narrow cave like a star.

Hades shrugged her shoulders, smiling the shy smile that always made my heart stop, tumble, skip.

"It's…silly, but it's what I do. My official use here." She tossed the sphere lightly, and it rose, floated, and then drifted back down to cast a yellow glow on her hand. "I create light for the Underworld."

"You do more than that," I insisted, but her soft eyes were unfocused, far away, and I wondered if she'd heard me. I remembered watching her dance with the light. I remembered dancing with her under a shower of stardust. How cruel, to bury her brightness in the darkest place. Though, I had to allow, no place needed her light more.

At last, we came to the end: the corridor fluted out into a small arching room of glittering stone. It felt safe, cozy. The ceiling rose over our heads to a single sharp point; if I stood on Hades' shoulder, I could have touched my fingertip to it. Before us there was a depression in the stone, a pond brimming with still water, reflecting Hades' light. I stood at the edge of the bowl and gazed at my own reflection—I looked different, but I recognized myself, perhaps for the first time.

Hades knelt down, tilted her head back, arms curving upward, as if embracing. I sat beside her, careful not to make a sound, and I watched her, mesmerized.

The goddess of the dead, my goddess. Love radiated from her face, a love that broke my heart in its purity, its totality.

"Beloved Gaea," she said, whisper soft, "beloved earth mother, please…come unto me."

A heartbeat, two heartbeats, three… There was a ripple upon the silver surface of the pond, a lucid thing, a luminous thing, spiraling ever outward. And, from the water, she came.

Like Charon, she shimmered, shifted, so that I could never make out her form, the outline of it or the features of her face. But she was as unlike Charon as could be imagined; her aura pulsed with love.

She filled the room. She was everywhere—
she *was* the room, the ceiling, the floor. She was
Hades, and she was me. Before us, suspended, was a
changing spiral of color, of beauty, of earth and sea
and sky and a mass of stars, the perfect pattern of a
leaf; and the beauty of a stag, dying; and the splendor
of a swan, rising up. There was everything within her,
everything that had been, everything that yet would
be part of the planet. I understood, in that moment,
the smallest truth of all that was, and it was still too
big, too awe-full for me to bear. I wept, and I pressed
my face to the floor, and my heart burst open, love
waterfalling from the hole there.

"Child." The word surrounded me, embraced
my shoulders, and there was such beauty in its
syllable, such wisdom and empathy and compassion.

"Yes," I whispered, closing my eyes to the
storm of color, the riotous burst of life occupying this
small space, and my small body. My chest ached at
the splendor; it was too much.

"Persephone." A gentle hand touched my
shoulder, and I turned—wordless, wide-eyed—and
reached out to her. She was warm, like the sun, soft,
like the soil, and gentle, like Hades' kiss. She
gathered me into an embrace and held me close. She
smelled like my mother, but deeper, older: wet earth
after a rainstorm; new baby leaves, the first of spring;
rich harvests of berries, grapes, grain. "Persephone,
Persephone," she whispered and kissed my forehead.

She looked like a woman now, her glory
contained in a vessel, a body like mine but not like
mine. She was round, curved, voluptuous. Bountiful..
Her hair fell to the ground and was every color on the

earth, her dress perfectly woven from the green of ferns and mosses. Upon her face shone the kindness of every person, every creature which tread upon her world, herself, and it was too beautiful for me to understand. I fell to my knees before her, and her smile created me anew.

"My child, I have dreamed of you."

"Of…me?" I whispered.

"You." She reached out her hands and cupped my face gently. "You will change *everything*."

I gaped at her, uncomprehending. And then Gaea sank down before me, drew me to her, gathered me into her arms like a mother takes her child. "You are so loved, Persephone." And the love, like a wave, washed over me, lifted me up, filled me. "You will endure such sorrow, but you will transform the world."

In my heart, now, I felt the depth of future pains. I gasped, breathless, and twitched upon the ground as Gaea watched, her eyes brimming with the blue waters of her seas.

"You are destined for heartache, but also triumph, Persephone." Two shockingly blue tears fell from her eyes. "You—both of you," she said, taking my hand, Hades' hand, and joining them together, "are part of a very old story, a story that has and will always withstand the test of time."

I gazed at Hades; she glowed with love for me.

"It was foretold," Gaea smiled, watching us together. "Persephone, your descent was foretold. And you, Hades… Your souls were one long before there was an earth to be born upon. Millennia later, they are come together again, whole. All of this—"

She held out her arms. "All of this has been foretold."

My mouth parted to ask her a question—the one that troubled me, sometimes, even when I felt complete, and so loved, in Hades' arms.

But Gaea knew my thoughts, and the solace of her voice quelled my worries. "Child. Let go. There was nothing you could do to save Charis. And Charis *is* at peace, Persephone. True, enduring, forever peace."

My heart still ached, and I knew I would carry the ache with me forever, but to know, truly, that she wasn't suffering, that she wasn't tortured by the memory of Zeus' crime... *Let go*, Gaea said. I had been waiting for those words, for this permission. I lay my hand over my heart, closed my eyes, thought of Hades freely for the first time, without the specter of guilt haunting my heart.

Our story had been foretold...

"Do you love my daughter, Persephone? Do you love Hades?"

I reached for Hades, then, but she wasn't there, and when I looked about me, I couldn't see anything; the light was gone. There was nothing but darkness. I swallowed, anxious, and drew my knees against my chest.

"Do you love her?" Gaea asked again, and her voice was gentle, but I felt the true weight of her words, heavy as mountains.

"I..." I faltered not from doubt but because the strength of my love for Hades made me forget all else: words, reason, thought. How could I express my feelings, when words were such thin, mortal things, and the love I felt was something vast, timeless and, truly, immortal?

But I had to respond in some way, so I whispered, lamely, "Yes. I love her with my whole soul."

"You speak the truth—a perfect truth." Gaea cradled my chin in her hands. "Never forget, Persephone: you already possess everything you need to endure the challenges that await you. But take care of yourself. And..." There was a note of mischief in her voice. "Keep your head above water."

I gasped softly, wondered if she knew of my misadventure in the Styx...

"I know, my child. I was there, with you, all the while. I blessed you then, as I am blessing you now, for all that you are and all that you will be. I love you."

Again, I felt her lips on my forehead, and my body filled with light—light, light, and love in every crack and corner of my core. I lowered, slowly, gently, to the floor.

"Persephone?"

I opened my eyes to a dear vision of Hades. Beneath the glow of her golden sphere, she bent over my body, her hair shadowing my face. Concern etched her dark brow. "Persephone, can you hear me?"

"Yes," I whispered, lifting a trembling hand to stroke her cheek. "I hear you, Hades."

She blinked at me, once, twice, her eyes gleaming with unshed tears.

We were alone in the cavern, and the waters of the pond were calm, as before.

I breathed in and out, my body pulsing with magic. "Hades..." I gulped, sat up, heart pounding. "Hades, she's...she's *everything*. She's...so...so beautiful."

I fell against her chest, and she cradled me close, rocked me back and forth.

"Yes, she is."

"I don't understand how Zeus betrayed her. How anyone could."

"I don't know," she whispered, resting her chin on the top of my head. "I... Sometimes I wonder if...if all of the tales of cruelty and violence, the ones I have always accepted as established history—are untrue. Were never true. I know, for certain, that some of them are lies. What if he invented them *all*? What if all Gaea ever *was,* was love? What if the story of the birth of the world as I know it was a lie, Zeus' lie? He told it to me, not Rhea or Gaea. He told us all.

"I've never asked Gaea about it; I trust and love her. I see and feel that all she is...is love. And it's enough."

I leaned against Hades, and she stroked my hair, and we sat for a very long time, stunned, healed, whole, broken, everything, all at once.

When we stood, finally, to go, I paused for a moment to peer down into the depths of the silver pond. Startled, I saw that I cast no reflection...but strange spirals swirled in the water, and, beneath my eyes, they coalesced into words, the written language of the Greeks.

"Danger approaches. Be brave, my daughter. Take heed of Charon, and ready your courage." As soon as they appeared, the words faded.

A cold dread seized my heart.

Hades smiled at me, held out her hand. "Coming?"

Grateful that she hadn't read Gaea's warning—she had enough to worry about, too much, and I cherished her easy smile—I turned and followed her, and the earth's music followed me, both of us, during our long climb back up to the Underworld.

"Hades," I questioned, when, tired and breathless, we reached the dark, familiar plains of the Underworld, "you said that you knew some of the stories were untrue... Which stories? What did you mean?"

She wove her fingers with mine as we stepped over the path. In the distance, the palace shimmered, glowing like the moon, and it seemed taller, somehow—yes, it *was* taller, and more lovely than broken, more light than dark.

I gazed shyly at Hades, and I lowered my chin to hide my smile.

"Well," she sighed, "so many of the gods' stories, histories, are exaggerations, revisions of the truth. So many... And Zeus is at the center of it all. He has convinced the mortals that he is a kind and just god. Granted, he has done...some good in the world, but he is too selfish to truly care for anyone but himself."

She sighed again, cast her eyes upward. "He spreads lies, Persephone, to the people of earth. Since the beginning, he's spread lies about me. He whispers in their ears, invisibly, so that they don't even know where the knowledge came from. Because of him, the mortals believe me a cold, ruthless, hardened...man."

I leaned against her shoulder for a moment, and then I brought her hand to my mouth, kissed the gold-dusted skin. "If they knew the truth about you, perhaps they wouldn't fear death as much," I said, my voice just above a whisper, "and then he would lose some of his sway over them."

She inclined her head noncommittally. "I can't guess at his motives. Mostly, I think, he finds these things amusing, amuses himself by telling lies, destroying lives. He's...a bully." She pushed her fingers through her long black hair.

"For some years, his favorite trick was the reversal of genders— He is so powerful, he can become anything, anyone; he only has to think of it, and it happens. And he went through a phase during which he came down to mortals on the earth in the shape of a woman. I think that gave him the idea... He began to toy with the genders of the gods in the mortals' stories, the ones they recited in the temples, and to their children at night.

"Cupid?" Hades shook her head. "Cupid is a woman, Aphrodite's daughter, not her son. Aphrodite was furious with Zeus for the confusion he caused— still is, I imagine. But he won't retract the lie. He doesn't care."

Hades fell silent; she walked with her eyes lowered, so that the lashes shadowed her cheeks. I moved my hand to her arm, concerned, and when she didn't respond, I tugged on her gently, coaxed her to stop and turn to me.

"What is it? You seem sad, all of the sudden. Hades?"

She sighed, looked down at me, looked away. "Our story—our true story—will never be known, Persephone. The lies will take root, and they will spread."

"What lies?" I asked, though I shook my head, fought the compulsion to cover my ears; I was afraid to know.

Hades placed her hands on my shoulders and spoke softly, her eyes on my eyes.

"To the understanding of the world above, I am a ghoulish, selfish man, who wants and takes whatever it is that pleases him."

My mouth was so dry; I licked my lips and swallowed. I could hear the rush of the river Styx, the whispers drifting from the village of the dead, just beyond us, and, loudest of all, the leaping of our heartbeats, keeping time together in a place with no other means to measure it.

"They believe I'm a man, Persephone, a cruel one. When they know you are here, when they piece together Zeus' furtive whispers, they will believe that I...took you, kidnapped you—" Her voice faltered, and I drew her close to me, my arms encircling her neck.

"Hades—"

"If I am a man, Persephone," she insisted, her mouth against my hair, "and I have taken you against your will, they will say that I raped you..."

I held her closer still.

"...and that I forbid you to leave." She bowed her head and drew back, lifted her eyes to mine, mournful. "My lovely, unwilling captive."

The words lingered between us.

"Hades."

She began to turn from me, but I held her, forced her to meet my gaze. "Hades, I didn't know... I wish I could—" I stared at her, open-mouthed, crushed by the pain in her eyes. "We'll make it right, somehow. I won't have your name slandered—"

"It doesn't matter," she murmured, and she

kissed my neck, her lips trailing upward, drawing a line of fire over the surface of my skin.

"Do you think, for a moment," she whispered, "that I would have done anything differently? That I could have chosen anything but this, now?" Her dark eyes were alive, bright, shining. "I would suffer any lie, Persephone, for you."

"Oh…" My heart broke and mended in the same instant, and I drew her head down, kissed her deeply. "I love you, Hades."

Her breath stilled, and then she was kissing me back, her mouth devouring mine.

"Yes," she whispered over and over again, crushing my lips with kisses, her fingers tracing my cheeks, my neck. "Yes, yes, I love you," she said, and I held her, a dream in my arms, and I was whole.

Ten: Uprising

"**P**lease don't go," I begged her, wrapping my arms around her neck, kissing her, laughing as she laughed and gently struggled from my embrace.

"I must, Persephone." With a raised brow, she held my mischievous arms at my sides and kissed me good-bye—kissed me until my knees gave way.

I dropped down to the floor, laughing, sighing, drawing my arms around my legs as she paused in the doorway and smiled softly at me.

"I'll come home to you as soon as I can," she said, voice hoarse, her smile slowly fading. As I watched, her eyes darkened—not with anger or grief or sadness, but…She gazed at me, at my mouth, my hands. Every part of me. My mouth opened; my heart stopped.

I wanted her, and she wanted me, and as she turned and left, I knew it would be tonight—it would be *tonight*. I lay back on the floor and stared at the ceiling, my head spinning, the whole world spinning. She was gone now. But tonight...

"You're so obvious," Pallas sniffed, stalking into my room.

I propped myself up on my elbows and gave her the most unapologetic grin of my life. She sat down beside me, shook her head, and grinned back.

"I'm glad," she said, earnestly. We lay down side by side on the cool floor, staring up at the veined patterns in the marble ceiling—as we sometimes did, when we were extraordinarily bored. Cerberus bounced around us, licked our toes.

"I've never seen her this happy," Pallas said. "Ever. It suits her."

My stomach twisted. Pallas—Pallas would never be happy, not with Athena. I wondered, could the dead love again? Could they find their soul's match here, in the darkness? Or would they always be haunted by the memory of the one they left behind? Waiting, biding their time, until they were at last reunited.

But if you loved a goddess—you would never be reunited. Goddesses never died, never descended to the Underworld. Save one.

"Sometimes," said Pallas, so softly, "I wonder if it ever happened at all. Why would Athena, the goddess of wisdom, love me?" She turned her head to the side, away from me. "But she did, Persephone. We met at night, and she loved me, and I loved her, so much."

She scrubbed at her face with her hands and

sat up. "We were a terrible match. I know that. But I would do it all over again, if I had the choice." She nodded. "I would."

She rose slowly, began to pace the room. I watched her, worried for her—she had become so transparent, she scarcely seemed real. Sometimes I had to touch her to assure myself that she still had substance, that she wasn't going to disappear.

I felt her pain, and I wanted to comfort her— but what comfort could I offer? I couldn't bring Athena to her. I couldn't give her back her life.

Still, I stood up, my head dizzy from Hades' kiss, and held out my arms. She waved me away, scowled.

"Anyway," she began, but I touched her shoulder, made her pause.

"If this had never happened, if you had never…come here, what would you have done?"

The question seemed to surprise her. "What do you mean?"

"You and Athena—what were your plans before…"

"Before it all fell apart," she whispered, sighing. She wouldn't meet my eyes. "I wanted to marry her."

"Marry her?" I blinked, curious, and she laughed.

"You don't know what marriage is?"

I shook my head. "I was sheltered, in my forest."

"Ah, yes. Well, it's something mortals do… It's a dedication, a lifelong one. Before the gods and their families, couples dedicate themselves to one another.

"Sometimes people marry for reasons other than love: a man desiring a wife might exchange money with her father, and she would bear strapping sons for the wars. But in the beginning, it was simple, beautiful, a vow of love before the gods."

She chewed her bottom lip. "I obsessed over it. It was what I wanted, more than anything." Sighing, she kicked her sandal against the floor and scoffed. "But it was absurd, a stupid idea. The ritual was for mortals, and with Athena being a goddess, what would we have done?"

Her head hung low from her shoulders. "I didn't care about the details then. I just...I wanted to be her wife."

"Pallas..." I rested my hand on her arm. "Pallas, it's not absurd or stupid. It's a *beautiful* idea."

"Well," she said, detaching me from her elbow, "it never came to anything, so it doesn't matter either way."

I followed her out of my room, down one long hall, and then another. "Did Athena know?" I called after her. She shook her head as she walked.

No, she hadn't known. Athena hadn't known what Pallas intended, or—I could only guess—how deeply Pallas loved her. And now she sat on Olympus, another mortal girl in the circle of her arms, Pallas forgotten.

It could never be fixed.

I felt the pain of it as if it were my own. If I were separated from Hades, worlds apart, forever, I... I couldn't even think of it.

"I'm expecting a visitor today, one I thought you might like to see, as well," Pallas said, smiling faintly at me over her shoulder as we passed through the main corridor and descended the front steps of the palace. "Care to join me?"

"Always," I called after her, running to keep pace. I slipped my hand through her arm, and together we began the slow, tedious trek across the Underworld plains.

"I thought no one came to the Underworld besides the dead," I whispered. "Who is this guest of yours?"

We moved among the outlying cave dwellings of the village. A young girl stood in a doorway, grasping a tiny doll sculpted of earth. Her eyes followed me, and my heart was racked with pity. These souls had little, perhaps nothing, to look forward to, or hope for.

"You forget who guides the dead down to the Underworld," Pallas reminded me.

"Hermes!" I gasped. "When will he be here? He won't cross over with Charon, will he?" I remembered Gaea's admonishments, written in the water, and worried for my friend.

Pallas shook her head at me. "No, no, of course not. He flies like a bird with those sandals of his, and, anyway, he's the one who taught me the string-and-boat trick. Perhaps he invented it. He *is* the god of tricksters."

I nodded and exhaled, relieved.

"What's gotten into you, Persephone?"

"Oh…" I sighed. "Hades took me to see Gaea, and Gaea warned me to be careful. She mentioned Charon, specifically."

"Charon?" Pallas seemed shocked at first, and then thoughtful. She remained silent for several long minutes, as we hurried through the village. Souls stared at us, glared, sometimes hissed, their whispers steeped in animosity.

Finally, when we were free of the village, Pallas dropped her voice, asked, "Did Gaea say why you should be careful of Charon?"

"No. But he hates me. I assumed it had something to do with that."

Pallas sighed. "Did Hades ever tell you the story of how Charon came to be?"

I shook my head, and we walked toward the river.

"Hades made him."

My heart dropped within me. "How... Why? Why would she?"

She folded her arms, as if chilled. "Gods—some of them—can create life, people and creatures, monsters."

I remembered the naïve conviction of my childhood that my mother had created me, grown me from a seed, like one of her flowers. But then she told me about Zeus, told me she wasn't powerful enough to make immortal life by herself.

But Hades was. Hades was more powerful than I'd ever guessed.

"Charon was the first, and only, creature Hades ever made. She was overwhelmed with all of her duties here; she needed help, and of course no god would volunteer to live and work in the Underworld with her.

"So she made Charon. He was supposed to be a man, a simple ferryman. But...something went wrong." Pallas frowned. "He was malformed, of body and mind. Hades felt terrible. But Charon was determined." Pallas turned to me with a sardonic smile. "He still wanted the job. He wanted to ferry souls across the Styx. It was what he was created for; before Charon, Hades brought the souls to the Underworld herself, and it consumed all of her time."

My head felt too full of shock and wonderment; there was no room left for forming thoughts. We walked in silence for a moment.

"I think he hates Hades for creating him," Pallas whispered. We were near the river now, and she cast her eyes about, as if worried that Charon might be hiding somewhere, listening.

Pallas groaned. "Honestly, I just wish something would happen to tip the balance. It's becoming too much to bear—the constant whispering, the accusations, the misguided hostility."

"Perhaps it's time to tell Hades," I sighed. "She knows the people are unhappy, but she's so busy, and she thinks the best of...everyone." My shoulders rose, fell. "She can't see it, and won't, until it's too late."

Pallas pushed her hands through her hair. "I don't know what to do. I don't understand why nothing I say to them sinks in. The dead used to be reasonable, and content with what they had, as little as it is... The mutterings only began a few months ago.

"Persephone," she whispered, stopping before me, speaking in such a low tone that I had to read her lips, "I think Charon is to blame for this. What you've told me today confirms it for me."

I twisted my hands, said nothing. The structure of the Underworld seemed to falling apart, and I felt helpless to do anything to stop it.

A flickering figure, a gathering of silver and blue light, appeared at the edge of the Styx, waiting for us. Pallas and I ran toward him, and he zipped through the air, closed the distance between us by half.

"Hello, most lovely of ladies." He bowed to me, then swept Pallas from her feet, embraced her in a theatrical hug. She played along, making flourishes with her hands and pretending to wipe away tears.

"He's too snobbish to come any further into the Underworld," she laughed, pointing to his perch on the rocky bank of the river.

"Not snobbish, just cautious." He surveyed the vastness of black behind us. "Remember, I led all of those souls down here. I'd rather not be recognized…especially now."

"Can you feel it?" asked Pallas, worry wrinkling her brow.

Hermes shrugged, shifted, hazed out of sight. And then he appeared behind me and leaned his tousled head upon my shoulder.

"Something is brewing," he said, lifting his chin, "but that's not why I'm here. Zeus has been telling stories again, and they're not pretty."

"What about?" Pallas regarded him with her hands on her hips, mouth set in a firm line. "Hades?"

"His favorite subject." Hermes' eyes darted between Pallas and me. Suddenly, he was kneeling at my feet and holding my hand. "Persephone, have you given any more thought to your personal rebellion?"

I tilted my head at him. "I have rebelled. That's why I'm here—"

"There's more to it than that." He shook his head slowly. "You spoke with Gaea?"

"How did you—"

He tapped his head, and I remembered his trick at reading thoughts. But then he flickered and was gone, and I turned to find him standing beside Pallas, though his eyes bored through me. "Did you speak with her?" he persisted.

"Yes." I balled my hands into fists. *It's beginning*, I thought.

"And what did she tell you?"

"You are destined for heartache, but also triumph. You will endure such sorrow, but you will transform the world."

I wrapped my arms around myself—aching for Hades' embrace. I stared across the Styx and held my tongue. I didn't know what Gaea's words meant, what anything meant, and part of me didn't want to know, didn't want anything to change. Because I was happy now, so happy.

"She blessed me," I whispered. "She told me that she loved me."

"And was that all, Persephone?" Hermes' gaze was intense; I looked away. I did not answer and did not lie.

Finally he sighed, frustrated. "You were meant for greatness, Persephone. Choose your path wisely."

I turned my back to him.

"Any news of Athena?" Pallas whispered, and Hermes regaled her with anecdotes of the goddess of wisdom, the clever words she'd spoken, and tender words, too. When Hermes told Pallas that Athena missed her, I abandoned my sulking and faced him again, narrowed my eyes.

Did Hermes lie, make things up? He enjoyed

tricks, I knew. But his affection for Pallas wasn't an act, and I was certain, if he lied, he did it only to preserve her peace of mind, and her beautiful smile. Perhaps I would have lied, too, if confronted with Pallas' hopeful eyes.

She thanked him, hugged him and then strolled by herself down the length of the riverbank.

Hermes approached me, and I sighed.

"My mother?" I asked him, steeling myself against his reply. For the most part, I had quelled my longings for green, for trees, for the meadows I had loved with all my heart, but my mother... I would never stop longing for her. Part of me missed her, but all of me loved her.

"No word," Hermes said. "Demeter has...disappeared."

I paled.

Before I could question him, he grabbed my elbow firmly, swallowed, his face devoid of mirth. "Something bad is going to happen here, Persephone. Are you prepared for it?"

Stomach tied in knots, my heart twisting, worried for my mother, for Hades, Pallas, myself, I nodded. "Whatever happens, we'll endure."

"How can you know that?" His flashing eyes searched my face. "You are not omnipotent. You're immortal, but you can be killed—here, Persephone. Especially here."

"I trust," I whispered, biting my lip.

"In what?"

I drew a deep breath, stared unseeing at his face, shame and exhilaration branding me with a hot red flush.

"Myself, Hermes," I told him, defiant, and my

voice shook, but it didn't matter, because I spoke the truth. "I trust in myself."

His mouth curved upward; I recognized in his impish expression the god I had first met on Mount Olympus, the god who had dared me to rebel.

"Then you have all you need," he smiled, and with a bow, he winked at me, and flickered.

One moment, he was standing beside me, waving, and in the next, he was gone.

My hair fluttered in a sudden breeze.

The Underworld is stagnant, lifeless. Nothing moves here, save for the walking dead and the river…but now, as I joined Pallas at the edge of the bank, a chill wind gusted, and it hadn't come from the water—it came from behind us, from the plains of the Underworld itself.

I turned, surprised, to face it. It had been so long since I had felt the wind. I clasped Pallas' hand, but her fingers were slack, and when I looked at her, perplexed, she was stricken, and more transparent than ever before.

"It is an ill wind that blows in the Underworld," she whispered to me, fear quaking in her eyes.

"Dark talk has turned you sour." I smiled at her weakly. My stomach hadn't settled from the news about my mother, and I trembled inwardly at the thought of the portended horrors to come.

"Let's go visit the horses—they always cheer you up."

"Not today, Persephone," she muttered. "I must return to the village. I have to try—"

"Pallas, it does no good, for them or for you." My words sounded harsher than I'd intended, and she flinched, took a step backward. "Come with me," I urged her. "Forget about sad things for a little while."

She gazed at me as if I had gone mad. "Hades doesn't forget things, Persephone. Every day, she goes to the Elysian Fields, and she does what she can, whatever she can. What do *you* do?"

The accusation shredded me, digging deep into my heart with poison-tipped claws.

I couldn't speak. I was stung—most of all, because I realized her words were valid.

I did nothing. It was true.

Spent, discouraged, she turned to go.

I could have called out to her, asked her to wait, but I didn't. Couldn't. I sat down on the edge of the riverbank, careless of my nearness to the teeming waters, and I watched her walk away from me.

As I sat there by myself, long after she'd gone, I began to feel angry. I hadn't asked for my fate, my birthright. I had chosen to leave the forest, yes. That was my doing. And Hades had never asked for anything from me, though she had saved me, perhaps saved my immortal life.

But everyone else, everyone I had ever known, wanted things from me, things I didn't feel capable of giving. Hermes believed I was going to do something great. Gaea had told me that I would change things. And Pallas...she thought I was lazy, uncaring, but the truth was simpler than that.

What if the only thing I wanted to do was live in the palace, quietly, learning every curve and secret of Hades' body, and of her heart? I wasn't complicated by nature. I had never desired power or possessions or fame. I just wanted to *be.* And to be left alone.

Sullen, I rubbed at my eyes, gazed at my hands in my lap, sighed.

I had never asked for any of this. But I had it, nevertheless.

Perhaps that was the cost of immortality.

Hades had never asked to be the goddess of the Underworld, but she was, and she carried out her duties faithfully, unfailingly.

Suddenly I felt very selfish, like a child throwing a tantrum.

Gaea told me I had everything within me that I needed. But I was so afraid. I was afraid of the dead, afraid of Zeus. I was afraid of a hundred million things.

Lost in my musings, I jumped, startled, when I heard the scream. I sat very still, the hair on my arms standing up, and I heard it again: a scream, a woman's scream, originating from the direction of the village of the dead.

I stood, slowly, and gazed at the sprawl of dwellings, far distant. A dark shadow was spreading over the land, and I closed my eyes and opened them, feeling the earth spin beneath me.

It wasn't a shadow; it was a gathering of the dead—thousands of them—their bodies pressed so tightly together that they looked like one dark rolling mass. Normally the dead were quite solitary; they stayed apart, minded only themselves, joining together only when something was happening, another riot or a summoning from Hades.

Another scream, and a shout. I thought I recognized the scream now, and dread coiled around my insides like a monster, a snake, squeezing.

Pallas. Pallas was in danger.

I ran, tripping over the hem of my tunic, so I yanked it up, looked at the fistfuls of white in my hands—a lucid moment in my terror. I ran, and I couldn't breathe, couldn't pull the air through me as the village of the dead drew closer and closer, the dead themselves closer still. They were moving toward me, roiling slowly, and they were silent, silent, as whisperless as buried bodies, as they stared at me, hollow eyes unblinking.

Pallas screamed again, and I saw her, in front of them all, dragged along by a row of men and women, kicking and cursing and struggling against them, clawing at their arms, but there were too many, and she was losing strength, because I could barely see her. She looked like a ghost.

I skidded to a stop before the horrible, creeping shadow, my lungs burning. Pallas looked at me, eyes dull.

Her captors, all of the amassed dead, looked at me, too.

"What are you *doing*?" I shouted, drawing myself up to my full height. The skirt of my tunic billowed down around me as I released it. "What are you doing to her?"

"Taking her to the river Styx, where she belongs," a woman barked, her stare defiant, her hands gripping Pallas' arm. She looked surprisingly solid, real, and I recognized her, had encountered her before, though she hadn't been as substantial then.

"You can't do that, Hageus," I said evenly, matching her fierce gaze with my own. "She'd be trapped forever in the river."

"She deserves it, worse, for speaking the gospel of Hades." She spit on the ground. "As do you, *goddess* Persephone." The wrath in her voice startled me. Almost too late, I backed away from her companions' grasping hands.

"You can't—" I tripped on my hem as I moved from them, just out of reach.

"We will. And then we will drown Hades, too." She sneered. "The thing about you gods? I've watched you. You're a lot like us. You may not die, but I think you could be trapped in the river, like the mortals. I *know* it. You'll be stuck there, and we'll be free. And the Elysian Fields will be ours." She laughed, arching her head back, mouth too wide in her thin, bitter face.

Spurred by her outburst, the dead raised their hands and cried out in one loud, chilling voice. There were no words that I could make out, just a grating, guttural sound. My skin crawled, and I backed away further still, shaking my head, balling my fists.

No, no, no. This was wrong, so wrong.

Gaea had saved me from the Styx. Would she do it again? Would she save Pallas and Hades? Would we three be lost there forever?

Hageus stepped forward, holding out her hands, grinning like a madwoman. She *was* a madwoman. I didn't know what to do, felt fear eating me from the inside out...

It was up to me now, I realized, in a brief moment of clarity, and I felt a strange peace descend upon me.

I had to do something, say something. I had to stop this. Change the flow. Change everything.

"She's told you the *truth*!" I screamed.

My voice tore through the tension, ripped it open.

Hageus paused. They all paused.

And they were all staring at me.

"The Elysian Fields is a place of torment and misery," I said, breathless, the words spilling out faster than I could think. Better not to think.

"The heroes that Zeus has favored sit beneath the sun, in an endless field of wheat—yes!—but it is no a haven. It is a prison. They sit, and they contemplate the horrific acts they've committed. They are captives of their memories. They dwell on their guilt, reliving it all, again and again, remembering the murders and rapes they carried out because Zeus asked it of them, because they wanted this eternal reward."

I strode before Hageus and glared at her pointedly. "It is no reward. There is no escape. Every day, Hades goes to the fields, and she tries to offer comfort. And she succeeds, sometimes, for a moment. But only for a moment. There is no peace there. And the beauty of the landscape is a cruel joke." My voice was shaking, with fear but, also, with passion. I closed my eyes, opened them again, and recoiled inwardly from my next words: "Let me show you."

Pallas's head jerked up, and then she was shaking it hard, back and forth, mouthing the word "no" over and over.

I knew her thoughts. I thought them, too.

If I took the villagers to the Elysian Fields, they would have access to Hades. Right now, she was safe. Hidden away, unaware.

But if I led them there, let them in… We would be powerless to stop them if they mobbed us. We would be at their mercy.

It was a chance. A choice.

My heart urged me not to back down, and I listened to it.

"You must see…" My voice rasped, cracked, so I tried again, shaking, but standing firm. "You will see, when I show you, that all Pallas has told you, all I have told you is true. Hades—" Tears formed in the corners of my eyes, and I let them fall, because they were tears for her. "Hades is a kind, just goddess. She wants nothing more than for everyone in her kingdom, all of you, to be content, at peace. She does what she can—she pushes herself to the breaking point—to ensure that." I narrowed my eyes at Hageus, at the people surrounding her, and I promised them, "You will see."

"Show us!" someone cried out, and then another; the words rose up in a chorus, deafening me with its urgent pitch.

Pallas regarded me with heavy lids.

If this plan failed, if it went wrong…we would lose everything to chaos.

I turned, resolutely, and marched toward the center of the plains of the Underworld, the place Hades had taken me to when she let me into the fields. A sea of the dead followed in my wake, dragging Pallas with them. I clenched my jaw and steeled myself to walk calmly, slowly, with the dignity of a goddess, but I faltered, tripped over my own feet, and every part of me was trembling. My mind felt jagged; I could find no solace in it.

What if sight of the fields didn't convince them? They clung so stubbornly to their false beliefs. Could they be swayed?

Would Hades be safe?

She had to be safe. That's all I wanted.

Hades needed to survive this. She needed...she needed...

My heart contracted. I didn't even know if I could find the fields. I didn't know how to open the door to it. Pallas had said that only Hades could open the door.

What made me believe that I could do it?

A feeling. A compulsion. A hope.

I had no answers, no guarantees, but I was determined to trust my heart. It was all I had left.

When we reached our destination, I said nothing, thought nothing. I fell to my knees, raised up my hands, and I prayed (who do goddesses pray to?). I said, "please," and I envisioned the Elysian Fields in my mind, remembered the way the sun had warmed my skin there, remembered the soft shushing of the wheat, and, most of all, remembered Hades—my Hades—kneeling before the grieving mortal on the ground, offering compassion and gentleness in a place that scorned her for it. I remembered the taste of my tears.

I tasted them again now.

My eyes were closed, and I was weeping, but when the change came, when the light fell over me, I wiped my hands over my face and rose.

Wheat, everywhere. Wheat and the dead, the dead I had brought here, and when I turned to look at them, I noted how different they looked in the light. They were translucent, and their eyes squinted, their backs hunched; few of them would meet my gaze.

Frightened. They were frightened.

I watched them, and I tried my best to understand them. They had wanted this for so long, had pinned all of their hopes to it. They didn't want the Elysian Fields to be a land of misery, as Pallas and I insisted it was. They wanted it to be a home. In the end, all they wanted was a home.

I found Pallas in the throng, and her mouth was sagging; she implored me with her sad eyes.

I shook my head, determined. This would work. It had to work.

"Come," I said, moving through the wheat, pushing the dry stalks aside, "and listen."

We walked, and the fields darkened around us, darkened with crouching bodies, and we heard their wails.

Sadness punctured my chest, wormed into my soul. I felt too weak to go on. I wanted to fall to the ground and give way to my own grief.

But I didn't. I thought of Hades and I swallowed my weakness, led the dead deeper into the wheat.

Some of the heroes looked up at us, wonderingly, with watery eyes and faces streaked with tears. Most of them failed to notice us at all; they were too lost in their sorrow, sobbing or screaming, or both.

As far as the eye could see, farther, as far as the illusion of field and sun stretched on (forever and forever), there was misery, pain, the deepest of sufferings: an eternity, with only regrets for companions.

I covered my ears to block out the keening, the weeping, but I could not bring myself to close my eyes. I turned around and regarded the dead villagers, noted their shock and their horror, and, worst of all, their disenchantment. Their loss.

They had been hoping for paradise, and now

they knew that there was no such thing.

Hageus stood, stunned. Her eyes found my face, and her mouth hung open, but she seemed incapable of speech. She gestured at Pallas, and her captors let her go.

She fell to her knees, and I hurried to her, held her up, smoothed the hair back from her face.

"Will it be all right now?" she whispered to me, leaning against me, her hands clasped around my shoulder.

"I think so. I don't know." I inhaled deeply. "But I think so."

We both turned our heads, surprised, when one of the villagers, a teenage girl, pushed her way out of the grey, mournful crowd. She wore a ripped garment; her dark hair twirled down the center of her back. She gazed at me for a moment, and I couldn't guess her thoughts—her eyes were so empty.

And then she did something astonishing.

She kneeled down before one of the heroes.

He was rocking on his knees, rocking back and forth, back and forth. He wore dented armor, and his face was too young to be so scarred.

"It's you," the girl told him simply.

He hadn't noticed her, not until she spoke to him, and now he blinked, as if waking from a dream, and gazed at her face.

"No…" His voice was high, small, like a child's. He edged backward, his heels scuffing in the dirt, but she grabbed hold of his wrist, whispered, "It *is* you."

And the man began to weep.

"Please forgive me… I never meant… I didn't know… I'm so sorry." He crawled to her, on his hands and knees, and pressed his face against the earth. "Oh, forgive me, please, please forgive me…"

I watched their exchange, dumbfounded. The villagers were silent as they looked on, too.

For a long moment, neither the girl nor the hero moved. Emotions flickered over her face in slow succession—surprise, fury, pain, melancholy—until, finally, her features smoothed, were blank. She stood up, and she looked down at the man's prostrate form.

"I forgive you," she said thoughtfully, forming each word with care.

The man slid up from the ground, sat back, looked up at her, blinking away his tears.

"I don't know how you could," he said.

"I've had a long time to think about it." Hesitantly, awkwardly, she leaned over and patted his shoulder. "I'm not afraid of you anymore. I'm over it." She almost smiled. "It's over."

I shook my head, amazed. They had known each other in life. And they had found each other here, and, perhaps, resolved their pain.

They continued to sit and stare at each other, the girl resolute and clear-eyed, the man astounded.

A cry rang out from the throng of villagers, and an old man—thin and tottery—emerged, tripped, ran, and threw himself down at the feet of another of the heroes in our midst. He gathered the boy—who had been wailing, screaming, unceasingly—into his arms, and he held him, whispered to him, until the boy was silenced, and the old man wept on his shoulder.

Gradually, like birds breaking from a flock, the dead dispersed, wandered off, searching for souls who had gone missing, or for those who had done them harm, perhaps taken their lives.

I witnessed, with streaming eyes, profound moments of kindness. A little girl offered a hug to a hulking soldier. A sobbing wisp kissed the face of a man who had lost his legs but still had arms to wrap around her and hold her close.

Forgiveness, sympathy, empathy, love. The outpouring of emotion made me weak-kneed. I had steeled myself for a war, and, instead, here was its opposite: peace, given and found. I sunk down beside Pallas on the ground, and we leaned against each other, heads bent, simply breathing.

"Persephone? Pallas?"

I looked up quickly, shielded my eyes against the imaginary sun.

"Hades." Everything I felt for her, all of the love in my heart, tumbled from my mouth in the shape of that one precious word.

She stood over us; I basked in her shadow.

"Persephone, what happened?" She knelt down, gathered me into her arms, pressing her mouth to my ear. I shook my head against her. I couldn't speak. If I told the story now, I would fall apart, and I had to keep my composure for a little while longer, until I led the villagers back, until I knew that we were all safe.

"It happened," was all Pallas offered, and when Hades looked at her with a tilt of her head and an arch of her brow, she added, simply, "And it's over. It's all right. Thanks to Persephone."

Hades' eyes roamed my face. "But—how—"

"Shh," I smiled at her. "It's all right." I drew her lips to mine, kissed her lightly, cherished the warmth of her, the scent of her, for a short moment.

Then I stood, hands on hips, to survey the altered Elysian landscape.

The screams, the moans—they had been replaced, for the most part, with hushed, murmuring voices. People sat in small groups and spoke quietly, sharing healing, or the beginning sparks of it. I was so weak with relief, I was uncertain what to do, but Hades rose and put her hand in mine, and that was all I needed.

"Pallas?"

I turned my head, cast my eyes about for the woman who had spoken. Hageus. Her gaze slid over the three of us, as Pallas stood up, beside Hades and me, and she grimaced.

"I wanted to…" Hageus looked up at the sky, squinting in the light. "I wanted to apologize. I was wrong. You were right. I'm sorry that I didn't listen to you. I'm sorry…" She sighed heavily.

Pallas stared at Hageus for a very long moment.

The dead uprising could have ended in ruin—for Hades, for Pallas, for the Underworld itself. We both knew this, felt this, a yawning abyss of alternate reality, of what could have happened, what almost did happen.

I squeezed Hades' hand and swallowed the lump in my throat.

Finally, Pallas lifted her chin and stated, simply, "I don't lie."

Hageus nodded, her expression remorseful. "But I know someone who does."

Pallas' eyes flashed. "Tell me."

"Charon—he was the one. He told us that Hades had a plot against us, that she put her friends in the Elysian Fields and shoved the rest of us in the village." She glanced at Hades, quickly looked away. "He said she was responsible for everything wrong with the Underworld, and that if we joined together, we could overpower her...end her...and we would have the wonders of the Underworld to ourselves."

Her eyes skipped over Hades' face again. "We were going to kill you. We thought it was the only way."

Hades' expression did not change, but her grip on my hand tightened. "Charon told you this, to do this?"

"Yes." Hageus shifted from one foot to the other uncomfortably. "He told us that you were cruel and that Zeus was kind, that Zeus wanted to make things better for us down here, that he wanted to assume control over the kingdom of the dead...to help us." She swallowed. "Charon told us how to kill a god. He told us to throw you in the Styx."

"Wait," said Hades, holding up her hand. "Go back...*what*?"

"I've told you all I know," Hageus sighed, eyes on the dirt. "We believed that the Underworld was a dark and terrible place because you made it that way, to torture us. But now..." She held out her arms, to the fields, to the souls surrounding us. "Now I know we believed a lie."

Hageus left us, and Hades, Pallas and I stood facing one other, stunned.

"Zeus is behind all of this," I breathed. "He used Charon like a puppet. He's trying to steal away your kingdom. Hades—" I stared at her, open-mouthed. "Zeus tried to kill you."

Hades held her head in her hands, and she

shook it, back and forth. "That's—no. He's done some terrible things, but…death?" She swallowed, whispered in a voice that broke my heart, "Where do the gods go when they die? It has never happened before. He wouldn't wish that on me. He couldn't—"

"Couldn't he?" Pallas whispered.

I offered my arms to Hades. She leaned toward me, and I embraced her, held her, as she stared over my shoulder at the fields, silent.

I was silent, too, but inwardly, I raged. Zeus would answer for this. Somehow, someday, I would make him cower before me, in the name of my love. I swore it.

When we left the Elysian Fields, Hades did not close the door to it, promised to never close it off again. It shimmered and shifted, a golden land in the center of the dark plain. Now the dead—the villagers and the heroes—could come and go as they pleased.

Hades had told me, once, that there were rules, that she was bound by Zeus' decree to keep the heroes in and the villagers out. But things had changed now. Hades had changed. Dark shadows crowded her eyes.

She walked with purpose before Pallas and me, and we followed, side-by-side, mute. Our feet carried us over a long straight path pointed toward the river.

Together, we approached the rocky banks of the Styx, and together, we waited for Charon.

And he came.

His boat bounced over the churning waters, aimed in our direction.

Charon knew. He knew, and he stood there as he always did, pole in his hand. His shape was dark, darker than the waters beneath him; the only hint of movement and color was the wretched blue eye.

It stared at us.

"What did you do, Charon?" asked Hades, and there was pain in her voice, but also power, anger. I shivered.

"I did what I needed to do to claim what is rightfully mine," Charon answered in a dozen voices, voices he had stolen from coinless, desperate souls.

Hades did not hesitate. She stepped onto the boat, slowly, deliberately. "I *made* you," she whispered. "You were my creation, fashioned by my own two hands, with my breath for life. And you betrayed me."

"What would you have me do, goddess? Bow down before you?" He laughed his horrible laugh. "You offer me nothing, and Zeus would make me a king of this place. I would have made a proper ruler. I would have shown them the true face of fear…"

Hades stared at him, her shoulders square, her fingers loose at her sides. "What do you want, Charon?"

"Power," he hissed, but she held up a hand to him and shook her head.

"No," she whispered. "Truly. What do you want? Tell me, and I will give it to you."
Pallas gaped at me, eyes wide, and I covered my heart with my hand.

Silence slithered, sinuous, and expectant, like a world holding its breath

Charon broke it with a single word: "Freedom."

Hades held out her arms to him. "You had it, have always had it. You could have gone anywhere, anytime. You could go now."

But Charon swirled, a maelstrom of unspent emotion. "I was created for no other purpose than to ferry this boat. It is all that I am."

"Charon," said Hades, "I made you complete, with a heart and a soul. You are not bound to me. You can step out of that boat at any moment and walk away, if you truly want to."

His voice was sad, surprised, when he whispered, "I do."

Without a word, Hades held up her hands, palms flat, and light collected between her fingers, forming a sphere that glowed so brightly I had to blink and look away.

When I could see again, Charon—the shifting, seething, foggy mass of him—was gone, replaced by a dim, wavering soul, a soul like any other in the village of the dead.

It had happened so quickly, and so silently. Charon stared down at his hands, at his feet, at his body, his mouth open but unspeaking. He stumbled from the boat, placed uncertain feet on the shore, and walked by Pallas and me without a glance in our direction. We watched him move, unsteadily, over the dark plains.

"Freedom," Hades sighed, returning from the river. "Such as it is."

She looked down at her fingers, still sparking with gold dust, and then held out her hand to me.

She was animated, brimming over with power and potential. Our eyes met, and I saw, felt, knew only love.

Treachery had been paid back with kindness: such was the rule of the queen of the dead.

"I'll have to build a bridge," she said.

Far in the distance, the palace gleamed, shifted, grew.

Eleven: Changes

We lay in the dark. I could hear her breathing, heard the drumming of my own heart, the shift of cloth on our skin, the movement of her hand, brushing back her hair.

I closed my eyes, inhaled the scent of her, the earthiness, the deep water, the underground green. It had been a long time since Charis (not truly, but it seemed a lifetime, and then, only a moment), and I felt so young, so unproven—what if I disappointed her? What if, despite everything else, I wasn't what she wanted, or expected? She had existed since the dawn of the world.

I shook my head, remembered to trust (I trust myself), and gently, so gently, I reached out in the darkness and drew her to me.

"Thank you," she whispered into my

neck, into my hair, as she gathered me in, pressed her lips against my skin in five, ten, a hundred places. "You saved my life, Persephone."

"I didn't..."

"You are, even now."

Fire, fire everywhere. I arched beneath her, skin on fire, and she traced patterns over me, ancient patterns, and I tasted glory when she kissed me; we moved like pillars of light in the darkness—we shone.

Hades worshipped me in her own chamber, held me, touched me, knew me. I closed my eyes and pressed back my head and cried out, once, twice, again and again, as she found secrets upon me, within me, that I had been keeping for her.

"Oh..." I whispered into her night-black hair when the star burst, shattered, into a thousand pinpricks of light all through me. I dug my fingers into her arm and moaned her name, and she stopped my mouth with a kiss like an ocean, a desperate, wanting kiss, and I knew, in that moment, that there was nothing but love in all the world, or under it.

We curled up, her stomach against my back, every inch of me a heartbeat, and our hair tangled together, and we lay in one another's arms, a mirror image of each other—two souls shining, uniting, complete.

~*~

I woke to the cold. I shivered and sat up, alone, dread weighing me down. Hades was gone. Had I done something wrong? The fear lasted for a heartbeat, because Hades, beautiful Hades, came into the room, her face alight, glowing like never before, and she kissed me on my mouth, my neck, murmured my name into my hair.

In that moment, I felt the change in me, an opening, a ripening. It felt good and right. I was becoming someone different from the girl who ran wild through the Immortals Forest, daughter of Demeter. I was becoming myself.

"I love you," Hades breathed against my ear, and there was a cough at the doorway. Pallas stood there, and I yelped and gathered my garments quickly, blushing, but she laughed, Hades laughed and helped me dress, and I found myself smiling, too.

"Incorrigible," Pallas sighed, rolled her eyes. She had regained her solidity overnight; there was nothing wispy about her. She beamed at us, shook her head and left. We heard her laughter echoing in the hall of the throne room.

Hades turned to me, her lashes lowered, her mouth curved. "This, I promise, has nothing to do with last night." She took my hands, kissed them both, and guided me to my feet. "Though I must admit, I have perfect timing." Her smile melted something inside of me. "Come. I have a gift for you."

"Another monstrous child?" I laughed, as, half clothed, she dragged me out of the room, down the hall, and then down another. Cerberus, ever loyal, followed us around every twist and turn, and suddenly, impossibly, we spilled out of the palace— no, there was no palace behind us, only the Underworld plains, and before us, over us, towered a set of great double doors sunk into an earthen wall. They were intricately carved of a flashing stone; as we approached them, they changed color from black to brilliant green to cobalt blue.

I stared at Hades, speechless.

"Watch," she said, and she opened the doors.

My heart fell away within me, and I stepped inside, awed.

It was the sun…but it wasn't. Above us hung a globe that turned on a heavy chain, encrusted with tiny, glittering, golden gems. Hades must have hidden one of her golden spheres within it, because it flickered with light, cast off and fractured by the crystals.

And below, in the room, everything was covered with the little jewels, and I laughed, for there was a tree, as tall as I was, made of metal, covered with gems. There were flowers, perfectly formed and gleaming—not living, not real, but so vibrant that I imagined I could smell their sweet scents.

It was a garden of metal and stone. Trees, flowers, sun. And sky—the walls and ceiling were encrusted in crystals of a bright blue hue.

If I blurred my eyes, I could imagine I was standing in the forest again.

"Do you like it, Persephone?" Hades asked me.

I turned to her, tears in my eyes, heart so full I felt it breaking.

"Yes, yes, yes," I cried, pulling her against me, kissing her with the passion of a growing thing for its sun.

"How did you do this? Why—"

"I call it a sun room," she smiled, laughing. "Pallas helped. Does it remind you of your earth? Is it similar? Close? Close enough? Does this make you feel more at home?"

"Oh, Hades, you... You created this for me, to make me happy? Hades, I'm already happy. So happy. You're too good to me."

"Never," she whispered, drawing both of my hands up, kissing the palms so tenderly, softly, it was like a whisper. I shivered, and she drew me close.

"You have made of my life something beautiful," she said. "I am blessed beyond measure by your presence, and love... And I will spend the rest of my forever making you happy. I promise you that."

It was a bold, shameless declaration, and I folded her into my arms, drew her mouth down, kissed it until I couldn't breathe and my heart beat too fast.

I didn't want anything but this moment. Could we live for an eternity like this, sequestered away, untouched by all other fates save the one we created together? I didn't want to ask these questions, didn't want to think about the possibility that our lives could ever change. I wanted to live in this moment, this golden, perfect moment, for always and forever. I wanted Hades, here, now, and nothing else in all my life. I could be content forever, until the stars fell and the world ceased to be.

I held my goddess against my heart, willing time to spare us, to release us—two small souls— from its relentless, forward march.

"Hades, Persephone," Pallas said, and we both turned, surprised to find her standing behind us. The smile faded from my face as I took in the sorrow of her expression.

"What's wrong?" Hades asked her.

"Hermes is here. He needs to speak with you, Persephone."

My stomach contracted; my heart froze.

The moment was lost.

I knew why he'd come.

The path to the sun room, the hallways of the palace itself, had seemed so long and winding—but we traveled them too quickly now. Hermes waited for us in the throne room—Hermes, who never ventured beyond the banks of the Styx. He sat on the floor, legs crossed, his face grim, withdrawn.

"It's Zeus," he said, without a greeting.

The name provoked a violent tremor within me. I leaned against Hades, who stood behind me, and she wrapped her arms around my body, across my chest.

"He got to Demeter. She's made an ultimatum, Persephone. He knows where you are, has known for ages, and when he told her, finally, he must have spun more lies." Hermes paused, bit his lip.

"She has frozen the earth, and she has vowed to freeze the world in a forever winter if you do not return. She will not allow anything to grow. In time, the earth itself will die. You must return in three days' time."

Oh, Mother. Oh, Mother, Mother, Mother. Zeus spun no lies, didn't have to. He's hurting you; I know he's hurting you. He wants me back, and it terrifies me so much, because I don't know why, and you can't stand up to him, Mother, because he's the king of the gods, and he gets what he wants. I left—I ran away because he forced me to, and now he wants me back. But, Mother, I can't go back, not now. Not ever. I love her, mother. I love her so much.

I sunk down to my knees and collapsed on the

floor. I forgot to breathe, and it didn't matter. I covered my face with my hands. It was too much, too much, everything, all of it. It was too bright and too dark and too painful, and I had fallen in love and could not bear to leave. I would die if I left. For a moment, I wished I could die, because then I would have to stay here, with Hades, forever, and Zeus would have no claims to me.

"I'll go," Hades said, stooping over me, touching my shoulders with her gentle hands. "Persephone, please… It will be all right. I'll go—I'll talk some sense into Demeter, tell her the truth of what's been happening, which I'm certain Zeus left out, or distorted." Her mouth was set in a firm, hard line. "I'll go, and you'll see—she'll change her mind. I'll fix this."

I laughed, then, a sad, hopeless laugh, shaking my head, but the words wouldn't come, the words to tell her that she was mistaken, that my father was forcing my mother, that this wasn't my mother's doing at all…

"You have been down here for six months, Persephone," Hermes told me.

I blanched, put my hand over my mouth. It had seemed like days or weeks, not months—but time paced differently in the Underworld.

"If you don't come up, Demeter will freeze the earth so deeply that it will never thaw. People, everything, will die."

"It's Zeus, not my mother," I insisted, standing, drying my eyes, though I didn't remember crying. I turned to Hades and nearly crumpled again; she looked so lost.

"Hades…" I squeezed my eyes shut, forced

out the words. "I'll go up, and I'll explain—I'll explain everything." I wondered where my resolve had come from, but I swallowed and carried through with it. "I'm not afraid of Zeus. He has no power over me, not anymore."

"The moment you leave the Underworld, the moment that your feet touch the earth," Hades whispered, gripping my arm, "Demeter will sense you. She will find you. And if Zeus is with her, nothing that you say will sway him. He...he may keep you against your will. Or worse.

"No, Persephone—" She looked at me, and I fell into her eyes, wanted to lose myself to their darkness. "It makes the most sense that I return with Hermes, that I seek out Zeus, and your mother, too. I can mend this. I will."

I buried my face in Hades' chest, and my heart broke. "What if you don't return? What if this is what he wanted, all along? Zeus tried to kill you."

"What?" Hermes asked, alarmed. But Hades shook her head, stepped back from me.

"Trust me," she whispered. "I'll be back in three days."

Her motions were slow, prolonged, as she kissed my brow, my lips, held my hands, and then let them go.

She turned to Hermes, nodded at him, and— with a flicker—was gone.

It was so sudden. I couldn't believe it. My chest felt empty, as if my heart had gone with her. I sunk down again, pressed my forehead to my knees, commanded myself not to cry. But how could I exist without her? I couldn't fathom it. And it was only three days.

"Don't despair, Persephone," Pallas whispered, crouching at my side. She was shaking, shaken, but she did her best to comfort me. She offered her arms, and I fell into them.

From perfect joy to total anguish—I shivered, chilled bone deep, from the shock.

Pallas helped me to stand and rested her hands on my shoulders. "Please don't cry. It would break Hades' heart to see you like this. She'll talk sense into Zeus, and it will all be fine, just as it was before. You'll see."

Her intentions were good, but she sounded unconvinced.

I shook my head, scrubbed fists over my eyes.

Every possibility held its breath now. Anything could change; anything could happen.

Had I truly thought that, if I buried myself deep enough, I could escape it all, my destiny, my fate?

The torches on the walls began to sputter and fade. We were cast in a dim, grey twilight.

"When Hades leaves," Pallas whispered, "the light goes with her."

The light, my light, my Hades… She was gone.

Cerberus padded into the room, sat down in the center it, arched back all three of his heads and howled.

And then…the darkness was complete. Hades had left her kingdom.

There was a hole in my heart, and it could not be filled.

~*~

"The dead...how are they now?"

Pallas ran her fingers through her hair. "They're well. They wander in and out of the Elysian Fields, have formed into little groups, families."

"Has it all been peaceful?"

"Surprisingly, yes, it's been peaceful." Pallas held a faceted crystal in front of her face, examined it. "Death opens minds, sets some things right. Once they were able to face their pain, forgive, the grief fell away. But there are still mourners, still wails. Charon has hidden himself away in the fields; I've glimpsed him there, and he looks..." She shivered. "But nothing ties up perfectly, in the end."

We sat in my sun room, cradled in two gem-encrusted chairs that sparkled by the light of our oil lamps.

"You know..." I said, then, surveying my tiny, glittering garden, "I think it would be wonderful for the dead if they could come here, spend some spend time in this place."

Pallas shook her head, frowning, but the idea had taken root within me. "Oh, Pallas, why not? We could go to them now, show them the way, tell them they can come here whenever they wish, ask if there's anything else they need."

"They're dead," Pallas pointed out gently. "They need everything you can't provide."

But I stood up, determined. I needed to do something, to be busy, useful. Anything to dull the pain. "Come on, please. Let's try."

She followed me, sighing, to the village of the dead. The memory of the uprising, only days ago, lingered with me like a nightmare. I hadn't forgotten, would never forget, that they had intended to kill Hades. But I stood in the center of the village, and I stood tall, and the gathered onlookers, many of them carrying oil lamps in their hands, pressed closer so that they could hear me—Hageus, as always, front and center.

"Hades has built a beautiful place," I told them, my voice steady, as I gestured in the direction of the sun room. "Within it is a garden, a sky, a sun made of gems—like a glittering piece of captured earth. I would like to share it with all of you. This is your kingdom, too."

A long moment followed of practiced, calculating silence. Pallas, beside me, stood stiffly, watching the souls with a suspicious eye.

Hageus stepped forward, held out her hand, palm up to me. I gazed at her, bewildered. And then another person, a man, stepped forward and made the same gesture. Another, and another, and another— they all came before me, held out their hands to me.

Pallas gasped. "They're offering their loyalty to you, Persephone," she whispered in my ear. "Acknowledging you, officially, as their queen."

"They don't have to do that—you don't have to do that…" I shouted to the crowd. But they remained, unmoving, eyes on me.

"Accept it, graciously," Pallas muttered to me, shaking her head. "Say thank you."

"Thank you," I called out, undone, and, as one, the dead shouted my name.

They dispersed in separate directions, some wandering toward the far wall of the Underworld and the sun room, some approaching the distant, shimmering door that was the entrance to the Elysian

Fields. It shone like a star, a star inside of the world. It gave me hope. Not peace, but hope.

~*~

"Pallas," I said to her the next morning. We lay on my pallet, staring up at the marbled ceiling.

Cerberus was nestled between us, sleeping, one head pillowed on Pallas' leg, one head resting on mine, and one uncomfortably positioned so that it was almost suffocating. I sat up and adjusted him, until I was certain all of his noses were breathing properly.

"Do you remember when you told me about marriage, and how you had wished to marry Athena?"

"Yes," Pallas said, with trepidation. She sat up. "Why do you ask?"

"Well, I think…I think I want to do it, Pallas."

"Oh, I thought you'd never ask," she laughed, poked me in the ribs. Cerberus woke up, and we wrestled with him, ruffled his panting heads.

"No, I really—I know I want to do it. Do you think Hades would like to marry me? If I asked her, do you think she would say yes?"

She swatted at me good-naturedly. "She would travel to the stars if you asked her to fetch you one."

I smiled.

"She will say yes, Persephone. You plan on doing this, truly?"

"Yes," I said, my heart beating fast. "When she returns, I'm going to ask her to marry me."

"But you don't know the first thing about…"

"But *you* do," I said, grasping her hands. "Pallas, will you help me? Would you help me with the rituals?"

She nodded slowly. "I'll help you." Her face clouded, thoughtful. "But many of the Greek rituals involve the partaking of food, and we have no food in the Underworld. We have water, but I doubt either of you would be interested in drinking the Styx." She wrinkled her nose. "What could we use?"

I opened my mouth and shut it, skin prickling. "A pomegranate," I whispered. "I have a pomegranate. It's the only thing I brought with me from the upper world. Oh, Pallas, I have a pomegranate!"

I fell off the bed and reached up and underneath it. The pomegranate was harder now, but, as we stared at it, I knew that there was some magic to death in the Underworld, because the deep red fruit looked far better than I had expected it would. Just slightly overripe.

"It'll do nicely," Pallas said. "But, Persephone, marriage—it lasts forever, and what if you can't—" She caught herself, bowed her head, and then looked up at me apologetically.

I knew what she meant. What if I couldn't stay here with Hades forever?

"It doesn't matter. My heart will only ever belong to her."

I was still afraid, but I had realized some truths during Hades' absence. Even if we were apart, we would be bound by love. Everything else could change, on earth, below it, above it, but my love for her was fixed, like a star.

"We should do it in the sun room," Pallas said, waking me from my reverie. "I'll lead you both through the ritual."

"Thank you, Pallas. I need this. I don't know why, but I do."

"I understand, Persephone," she said softly, smiling. "And don't worry! She'll say yes."

~*~

I missed her so much, I couldn't make sense of the depth of it, the deep, dark pools of wanting that drove me to haunt the hallways of the palace each night. Before, I had wandered to her rooms, had gazed at the tree tapestry with her, had spent hours speaking with her in low, hushed tones—treasured words and moments that I had hidden away in my heart.

But now, now—there was an emptiness within me. Sometimes I doubled over, sick from the pain of it. Pallas kept me company, Cerberus always followed at my feet, a constant companion, and I loved them both, dearly—but they were not Hades.

On the third day, I stood in the throne room and paced. I didn't know when she would return, only that she would, so I would stubbornly wait, fretting, pacing, longing, aching, until she appeared. It did not occur to me that she might not return, that she might be delayed by something unforeseen. I believed her. She said she would come back to me after three days, and my belief was unwavering. I trusted her with all of my heart.

And she came.

She was weary, bone weary, but when she saw me, she crossed the distance between us, and she gathered me into her arms, kissing me softly, so softly. Light blossomed around the room, torches ablaze. But I backed away, looked into her eyes, and even before she opened her mouth, even before she said the words, I knew.

"Your mother," she began slowly, dully, each word like a sentencing. "She has nothing to do with this. Zeus...Zeus demands that you return, and he is using Demeter to control you. You must rise up tomorrow. The threat of eternal winter still stands. You must go, or winter will never end, and the animals, the humans will all die."

I felt as if I were made of wood, or stone. Part of me had believed, had truly believed, that Hades would succeed, that Zeus would back down, give up, find another distraction.

But the other part of me had been expecting this.

I couldn't understand the enormity of it, this future; it was yawning before me, a pit of blackness so deep that I couldn't see the bottom, couldn't see the horrors that waited, hungry, ready to devour me. Hades held me, and I did not cry, did not weep, only stood, impassive, a stone goddess.

Zeus wanted me back. Why?

"Persephone," said Hades, pressing her mouth to my hair, burying her face in the nest of curls. "Persephone..."

Hearing her speak my name was a thorn, twisting in my side, deeper and deeper until I cried out from the pain, until I sank down and down and down, until I sat upon the cold, marble floor, as small as possible, as if—in my smallness—all the troubles of the world would simply miss me, pass me by. I had journeyed here of my own free will. I had contended with Charon, I had figured out my own way of doing things, I had met Gaea herself, and I had helped to quell the dead uprising. All of this, *all* of this, I had done, had found the courage to do, had kept going, had not given up.

I had fallen in love. I had opened my heart, and I had fallen in love deeper and truer than anything I had believed possible. I had fallen in love with the goddess of the dead, and now we would be wrenched apart, apart forever. Hades was the queen of the Underworld—she belonged here; she had to stay here. She was safe here. She came up to my world so rarely...where I would be, and we were going to be separated, apart...

Oh, I could not bear it, and I let out a wail, and I beat my hands against the marble. Hades gripped my wrists, drew me closer to her, and I felt my heart break into a thousand pieces, shattering inside of my breast.

I knew Zeus, and I knew what he was capable of. If I refused, he would come here, for both of us.

He would kill Hades.

I had to leave.

"Persephone," she whispered. "My beautiful Persephone. Forgive me... I tried—I don't know what to do."

And we sat together on the floor, heads bowed together, touching, touching, we had to be touching, had to be close. This was all we had left, this moment, this day, this night. It was all we had, and once it was be gone, I would be gone, too.

"Hades," I whispered, "there's something I have to tell you—ask you."

She sat back, eyes dark and shining. And it was already broken, but I felt my heart break again,

again and again and again, until it made me sick, until I wanted to cry out from it. I swallowed, pressed my hands to my eyes, and opened them again. She was still there, still gazing at me.

"Hades," I whispered, taking her hands, pressing them together between mine. They were so warm, so soft, so real. "My beloved Hades, goddess of the Underworld, queen of the kingdom of the dead…" I tried to smile, but my mouth had gone slack. "Hades, would you please marry me?"

Her lips parted, and she sat for a long moment, speechless, as my pulse raced, pounded, waiting. But then she gathered me up and kissed me once, twice, three times, and said with fervor, "Yes, Persephone. I will marry you."

In that moment, in that precious, tiny, infinite moment, there was joy. I held it to me like a gem, held it close to my heart, tucked away, kept safe.

She would marry me.

"*Tonight*—marry me tonight," I whispered, kissing her.

"Yes," she said.

I went to my room to find the pomegranate. The long, low bed where I slept, the white marble walls—this had been my home. But I would not be sleeping here tonight. I wouldn't see this room again. I pressed my hand against the place where Hades had lain beside me, and I said a quick goodbye, my first goodbye, and I didn't look back when I left, pomegranate clutched to my heart.

I searched for Hades.

She was not in the throne room, and she was not in her chamber. I wandered through the hallway until I came to the front steps of the palace. Hades sat on the steps, staring up at the vast, immeasurable ceiling of the Underworld, at the blackness that covered us both.

"I stayed at Olympus while I was gone," she said, as I sat down beside her. Her eyes were fixed on the darkness. "The stars are the one thing that I miss about the earth. They're so constant, steady, bright. I've always loved the stars. You remind me of them, Persephone," she added quietly.

"I do?" I pillowed my head on her shoulder. She drew me close, her arm about me, holding me, caressing me.

"Yes..." she whispered, swallowed, fingered the hem of my tunic nervously. "You see, I have been content with the darkness. But then you came, with your fire. And you reminded me about the stars, shining in the dark, never wavering."

"Oh, I have wavered..." I argued, but she shook her head.

"You have been brave. You have done your best. In this, in all of this, you have done your best. How many can say that? You have made such a difference here." She smiled to herself. "Pallas met me at the Styx, walked back with me, and she told me that you opened the sun room to the dead. I don't know why I never thought of such things. In the time you've been here, you've changed...everything. I'm no longer needed in the Elysian Fields because you opened the door, and the dead themselves began to help one another." She swallowed again and looked at me fully. "I was blind. You opened my eyes."

I stared at her, blinking back tears. "Hades...how can we do this? How can we possibly do this? I can't...not without you...I can't lose..."

The tears were so dangerously close to falling, falling, ruining everything, these moments that were our last, that I was determined to spend joyfully. She shook her head, wiped the wet streaks from my face with a feather touch.

"You have been so brave, Persephone. You have done what no one else can do. You will be brave, still. You have enough courage to see this through—for both of us."

"I don't want to see it through. I can't do it, Hades. I can't go up there. How can I? Why must I?" The heat of my words shook me to my core. I didn't have to go up—*why* did I have to go up? Why did the fate of the mortals, of the world, depend upon me? I didn't want that responsibility. I didn't want to care. Why couldn't I stay? Everyone died eventually, anyway, and the Underworld was dark but safe, and far from the gods and their tricks and games.

And perhaps Zeus would forget. Perhaps he wouldn't come for us.

In that moment, selfishness consumed me, and I descended into the belly of the beast, resolute. No, I would not return to the earth. I would stay here and continue to make choices that guided my own destiny. Mine and no one else's. I owed nothing and no one, and I would do what I wished.

But even as I thought it, even as I tried to force it to make sense, I knew I wouldn't, couldn't follow through. Zeus had threatened the lives of every being on the planet. Would he really do it, twist my mother to his will so that she froze them all to death?

Yes, he would.

I leaned back against Hades' shoulder. She gazed at me silently.

"I loved the stars, too," I said then, and it felt like a prayer. "The North Star would be there." I pointed upward. "It is there, still shining—just...far away."

"Yes," Hades murmured. She sighed. "I can come to visit you, Persephone. And, perhaps, you can visit me, too. And this won't be forever, surely. Surely, you can convince Zeus, talk some sense into him, over time..." Her voice faded, and she added weakly, "Surely."

"Yes," I agreed, doubtful.

"Persephone...Hades?" Pallas appeared on the steps behind us. I rose, wiping at my eyes, offering my hand to Hades, who took it, rose, too. Pallas smiled, a smile that didn't quite reach her eyes, and spread her arms wide to the both of us. "It's time," she said, "if you're ready."

Everything was happening fast, too fast. I had never envisioned myself in this moment. I had never imagined I would find myself here, at the beginning of goodbyes. But, *no, no, no, Persephone*, I thought to myself, furious, as we followed Pallas through the passageways. If I kept my head in the moment, if I was only here and only now, that would be all that mattered, all that could touch me. Not tomorrow, not all of the heartache and pain that had come before, and would surely follow after—no, nothing but this moment would be real. I breathed in, and I breathed out, and as Hades threaded her fingers through mine, clasped my hand, squeezed—once, twice—I breathed in and I breathed out again, and I vowed with all of my heart that I would stay here, now, and let each moment come and go as it would. It was all I could do; these moments were all I would have, all any of us had, and I needed to begin by treasuring them with the honor they deserved. Here. Now.

Pallas had prepared the sun room for the ceremony, our ritual. Now, as we entered it, I saw two deep, marble basins on the floor on either side of the entrance, each of them filled with clear, bright water—from the pool in Gaea's grotto, I guessed.

Solemnly, Pallas gestured to us and to the basins. Hades let go of my hand, and I felt a shock, felt the cold creep over my fingers where she'd been and was now gone, but I steeled myself, closing my eyes, breathing in and out. I was nervous as I stood before my basin, and I looked over my shoulder at Hades.

She drew her hair around and over her right shoulder; it cascaded down her side, over her breast. Slowly, eyes closed, she shrugged out of her garments, left them in a small pile, stepped down and into the water, naked. She was so beautiful, the curves of her, the swells and gentle crests of her sacred body. Pallas turned and looked to me, nodding.

My hands shook as I, too, shrugged out of my tunic, careful to keep the pomegranate in the palm of my hand. I stepped into the basin, and I shivered at the cold.

Hades knelt down, splashed the water on her face, over her head, over her skin, and I tried to mimic her motions, realizing the intent of this rite—it was a cleanse, a purification, to make us new and worthy of one another, and of our promises, our vows. I trembled, and I felt changed when I stepped back onto the marble of the palace floor, naked, newborn.

Pallas handed me a red dress; to Hades, she

offered a black one. We donned these clothes and stood, gazing at one another. Black and red, Hades and Persephone.

"We begin," said Pallas in a soft whisper. Hades and I clasped hands, standing before her.

We passed a long moment in silence, gazing at one another, my heart stilled, quieted. My eyes drank her in: her long, straight nose, her soft lips, her dark, liquid eyes. I memorized her, every inch of her. The way that her neck curved down and in to the two bones, fragile as birds, that met in the hollow I had pressed my lips against, tasted. I memorized the gentle gaze that she reserved just for me, and I memorized the way that she looked at me—now—her eyes flashing, when she wanted me, desired me with all her heart.

"We stand in a room built of love," said Pallas. I clung to her words—they were real, they were now, they would keep away the future. "We stand," she continued, holding out her hands to us, "at the threshold of a transformation. Hades, Persephone, have you come here to marry one another, to profess to each other, and the world itself, that you love with a true love, with a pure love?"

"Yes," said Hades, in a voice so soft, so low, that it made me shiver.

"Yes," I whispered, and I cleared my throat and said again, firmly, "Yes."

"All you need to begin something is the courage enough to begin it," said Pallas simply. "Persephone, do you promise before yourself, before your goddess, that you will love her always?"

"I promise." My voice caught, and my eyes were gathering tears, but I shook my head, swallowed. I could not begin to cry, not now. I willed the tears back, stared into Hades' eyes—they were so dark, so full, so hungry.

"Hades, do you promise, before yourself, before your goddess, that you will love her always?"

"I promise," said Hades, her whisper washing over me like rain.

"As a symbol of your love, and a sealing of your promise, Persephone, what have you brought with you?"

I took my hands out of Hades', drew my fingers quickly over my damp face, and picked up the pomegranate.

"Partake of it together as an embodiment of your bond," Pallas said, and—with a soft smile on her lips—she bowed deeply to the both of us, turned, and left the room, drawing the two great doors closed behind her.

We were alone in the sun room, the created star sparkling above us. And in the corner, there was a wide, long, low bed—Hades' bed.

Pallas was full of wonders. She had thought of everything.

Hades sat down on the bed, gesturing for me to do the same. I was suddenly shy, the light from the sun illuminating every flaw I saw in myself, every weakness. I looked upon Hades, saw the strength and the beauty and unblemished character of her, the woman I had fallen in love with so deeply, and I wondered, silently, if I was enough for her.

"Come here," she whispered, and, drawing me down upon her, she reached up with her mouth, seeking mine. She kissed me, her hands pressing against my back, holding me in this embrace, comforting me, letting me forget. She kissed my cheek, my neck, as I shivered, as I whispered her name, trembling.

We lay together, side by side, and I held up the pomegranate. On a gem-encrusted table beside the bed, there was a knife, and Hades offered it to me. I sliced into the fruit. The red juice ran down my fingers, down my hands and arms, as I tore it open, and—never once taking my eyes from hers—offered her half. She took it, smiling, mischievous, and held it out to me.

I bent my head and lapped up a mouthful of the seeds. The thing about pomegranates is that they are sweet and sour—they make you shiver, as you devour them; they are sticky and red like mortals' blood, and you must chew them thoughtfully, carefully, a meditation on what it is to be a seed, to be courageous enough to grow inside a deep, dark fruit, waiting, waiting, waiting.

I swallowed the seeds, and I licked the palm of Hades' hand, even as she devoured her own portion. I let the knife fall to the floor, splattering the white marble with the juice of the fruit, and I lay down again, lay down beside her, red washing over me, red within and without of me. The red of the pomegranate and the red of my love mixed together into something deep, pulsating, a music only we could hear. I needed her, and she devoured my mouth, like she'd devoured the pomegranate, a sweet and sour taste between us as she pushed away my dress, climbed on top of me, between my legs, heart pressing against mine and breath hot against my ear, and I thought the crescendo would build within me until I shattered, every fragment of me too hot to touch or hold, feverish, fired, brilliant.

"I love you," whispered Hades, branding the words into my skin as she breathed them out here, here, hands pushing aside the bothersome cloth between us, finding my skin, gently touching, kissing. I arched up beneath her, because every single part of me cried out without words, crying out for her. I needed her to touch me, to whisper my name, to trace her tongue in wet spirals that glistened beneath the created sun. She bent down and kissed me, then, tongue between my lips, arm beneath my head so that I raised up to meet her, nestled, cradled as she ate me up, sweet and sour, the darkest of fruits.

Between my legs, she pressed down with her hips, pressing down and in, eliciting a moan from my mouth, a whimper. I begged her mutely to touch me there, to reach within me, find my great and terrible ache and fracture it into a thousand pieces. I was aware of every inch of her skin, of her body now, felt the curls of her hair tracing over my face and my neck. The scent of pomegranate and Hades filled me, and I closed my eyes as she kissed my stomach, lower.

I gripped the cloth on the bed and felt my heart leap against my bones when her fingers pressed down, curved up and in, questing, piercing me through and through and through, and there was a wave of shocking pleasure that rocked through me, and another, and had it been a lifetime or a heartbeat between then and now, because now, now, now, there was red everywhere and in everything, and I was opened, like a pomegranate, devoured, and she pressed her mouth to mine when I cried out, when the waves of delirium hit me, and her weight above me made it feel real, her pressing into me—we were not two, but the same creature, connected, bound. I put my arms about her shoulders and drew her down to me, her mouth to mine, as I shook from the crescendo, as I shook and shivered, and when it was done, when all I could do was lie there, weak, so weak, she gathered me to her, covered us both in a blanket, and nestled my head on her breastbone, a sweet smile on her lips.

There was a stain of pomegranate juice on her chin, and I traced it with a shaking finger, touched her lips, cherished the warmth and realness of her. Now that it was over (even though it wasn't, the reverberations of it still quivered through me, the most liquid light feeling I had ever known), it was *over*, and all I had was this moment where we were together, and how long would the night last, and I mustn't cry, I mustn't, but even as I thought, even as I did my absolute best to hold onto the moment of here and now, I lost it. I lost the string that connected me here; it snapped away from me, into the blackness, and I began to weep.

Hades said nothing, only drew me closer, pressed her lips to my hair, held me close enough that I could feel the pulse of her heart, beating beneath her lovely skin, against my skin. We were so close, I couldn't tell where I ended and she began. Now, on this night, we were one, and we would never—no, I couldn't use that word, never.

But I wouldn't delude myself. Did I really believe that Zeus would let me go, would ever let me go? Did we really believe that it was possible to build a life together under the shadow of a god who wanted to keep us apart?

It was too much, and I was too tired, and I wanted to be swallowed up by the darkness of the Underworld and sleep forever in Hades' arms, obligations obliterated. A long, immortal life of unhappiness lay before me, while my dark wife lived a world apart, alone.

"Persephone," Hades whispered. I turned to her, nose to nose, closing my eyes. I couldn't look at her. If I did, I would sob and never stop sobbing, and I wanted to do my best, I wanted to show her I was brave, as she thought I was. If I could be brave now, maybe she would believe I could be brave above, too, and then she wouldn't worry about me...

"Persephone," she said gently, touching my chin. I opened my eyes, took hers in—they were filled with such love, such kindness, that everything I was holding onto so tightly broke apart within me, and I was weeping again. How could we endure this?

"I know you think that it's over," she whispered to me, lips against my ear. I buried my face in her neck, drew my arms about her. "You think it's over, but it's not. I promise you, Persephone."

"How can you know?"

"I know," she breathed. "And I promise you this—we will be together again. I swear it. Do you trust me?"

It was a surprising question, and I looked at her, perplexed, tears spilling from my eyes. I pushed them away. "Of course I trust you. I love you."

"Then do you trust that I will find a way for us to be together?"

"Hades—"

"Persephone. Trust me. Have faith in me."

"I do," I whispered, heart breaking, numb.

"Please continue to trust me. I swear to you, I will make this right."

She waved a hand at the glittering sun over our heads, and it dimmed, softened. There was only darkness. I felt as if I had descended to another time and place. She was all around me, within me, holding me, part of me, now. She kissed me, gently, promised again that she would find a way.

And I didn't know how she could stop this, what she could do—there was nothing she could do—but I had faith in my goddess, faith in the possibility of something beautiful happening in my life, and remaining.

We came together in the dark, whole in one another, a marriage of the truest love, built upon a single dark fruit devoured.

Twelve:
Queen of the Underworld

It was morning; the glittering sun glowed. Hades kissed me awake, and for a moment, a very small moment, I forgot my pain. We were together, and we were married, and we lay in her bed in the room she had built for me, and everything was so beautiful. I wrapped my arms around her neck and drew her down to me, and then I *remembered*.

The reality of what was about to happen, of all that was about to change, lanced through me with such pain that I sat up, gasped. Hades gazed at me with heavy, hooded eyes. "It's going to be all right..." she began, but I pressed a finger to her lips, shook my head. If we stayed silent, if we didn't talk about it, this moment would stretch on and on forever, and we could stay here, we could—

The double doors scraped open; Pallas stood before us, looking very small, casting a long shadow over the room.

"Hermes is here…"

Hermes. Hermes had come to carry me across the river Styx, to fly me up the thousands of steps, to take me away, away—so far away.

It was over.

Hades and I rose. I gathered my red dress from the floor; Hades shrugged into her black one. I swept my hair behind me, tangled though it was, and—hand in hand, like children—we walked out, and we were in the palace, and we moved through the halls, found the throne room.

I stopped and stared. There were two thrones. The new chair was equal in size to Hades' black one, but white and carved with tiny vines and flowers and a scattering of stars.

It was meant to be my throne, as the second queen of the Underworld. A sob caught in my throat as I stumbled toward it, fell upon the seat, and when I met Hades' eyes, I saw the grief there, and it swallowed me up.

"Persephone," said Hermes, bowing low. He stood in the center of the room, the corners of his mouth turned down in a frown, and he held out his hand, hesitant. "Are you ready?"

I laughed, but it sounded like I was choking. I covered my mouth and crossed my arms in front of me, as if that could keep the future at bay. I would have given my hair, my eyes, my hands to Charon now, if he could have promised me *time*…time that I'd never had, time that always seemed to taunt me, running away too fast, leading me to caverns of the deepest despair and darkness.

The pomegranate was sweet and sour, and the sour taste now rose strong within me.

Hades took me by the shoulders, shook me gently. "Persephone," she whispered, and I looked into her eyes. There were tears there, black, shining. "Believe in me. Promise me you will, that you won't lose hope." On the last word, her voice broke, but she persisted. "Please. Promise me."

"I promise," I said, putting my hand over my mouth, angry, furious. I was being forced to leave, to leave *her*, and I was promising her something I could not do—to hold onto hope in a hopeless world.

"Here," she whispered, and took my hand. She pressed something smooth and flat into my palm. I turned it over, looked at the shimmering stone. It was deceptively dark, because when I turned it, it flickered blue and green, like the sun room doors. A long metal chain dangled from the top of it, strung with beads red as pomegranate seeds, and I realized that it was a necklace—Hades made me a necklace, something I could wear over my heart.

She took it from me, fastened it about my neck, and it felt so cold against my skin that I shivered.

"My link to you. I'll always be here." And she pressed a trembling hand to my heart, and she took me, roughly pressed her mouth to mine. I wrapped my arms about her, and we embraced, and we kissed, and I was weeping when we broke away. This, this, this was all I'd ever have, and it was ending. *Oh, please, please, don't let it ever end.*

Hermes held out his hand to me again. I took

it.

"I will come for you. I will. Don't give up on me. Please."

I turned back. Hades stood between our thrones, and she sagged, beaten, but her eyes still flashed. "I love you."

I nodded, tears blurring my sight of her. "I love you, Hades."

And Pallas was there, and she hugged me fiercely, pressing a note into my hand. "For Athena," she whispered, and I let her go, kissed her cheek.

I knelt and gathered Cerberus in my arms; he scratched at my legs, whining, whining.

And then I flew to Hades again. One last kiss. One last everything. Everything was breaking.

Hermes beckoned me, wrapped an arm around my waist, and I was weightless as he rose and shimmered, as I shimmered, too. Hades stood below, her lips parted as if she were going to say one last thing, but then she was gone, and we were already at the Styx, already beyond it, and we entered the great maw that took us to the corridor to the beginning—or end—of the world.

~*~

Light, light everywhere. I cried out and pressed my hands to my eyes. I was still, sprawled on the ground, and it was wet and so cold. I took away my hands, rose and blinked fiercely; tears streamed over my face.

Sunlight.

Hermes and I stood at the entrance to the Underworld, the opening that I had found and entered when I was someone else, a lifetime ago.

I stared, uncomprehending, at the forest surrounding me. The trees drooped, draped in glittering white. The barren ground was white, too, and hard as rock. A small herd of deer stood, terrified, on the edge of the clearing, watching us.

Everything smelled white, was white and cold and stark, and the *sky*—so blue, it broke my heart, made me gasp. But I didn't care about any of it.

I stared down into the Underworld…and the trees here, the earth, the beautiful sky paled and paled and paled and paled. This was no longer home to me.

"It's winter," said Hermes gently, turning me about, walking with me across the meadow, into the tree line. "Come…"

I walked, and it was all so bright, blinding, and I stumbled once, twice, across the trunks of fallen trees. Hermes caught me the first time, but not the second, and my hands landed in the white drift, the frozen water—snow, Hermes said.

I didn't get up.

I huddled there, shivering, for a long moment, my hands flat on the frozen ground. I was cold, and the wet seeped through my tunic, and Hermes was reaching for me, but I didn't get up.

And then something happened. Cracks spread in the ice, in the snow, beneath my fingers. And twining up and out of the cracks, on stems new and green, came flowers. They were white, with lovely bobbing heads and soft petals.

I stared down at them, uncomprehending.

The earth still loved me, still knew me, even though I'd abandoned it and had been gone for so long. It was a comfort. It calmed and centered me, though I carried a dead feeling in my belly, though I had left Hades and, with her, my heart.

And now, now, now I had to see my mother—and my father, the liar, might be there, too.

We crossed the Immortals Forest in moments, heartbeats, wingbeats, as Hermes carried me over the earth. We found my mother's bower too quickly, and I felt the earth rise beneath my feet as he nodded to me, face expressionless, flickering in and out and disappearing. He'd told me to rebel, and this was where rebelling got me, back to where I started, more broken than I'd ever been, alone, at the edge of a dark future.

I pressed Hades' stone against my heart—it was warmed, now, from the heat of my skin, and I thought of her, far, so far beneath the earth, and I took a deep breath, and I entered the bower.

"Persephone..." My mother gathered me into her arms and—so softly, I almost didn't hear it—began to weep against my shoulder.

"I'm sorry," we both said, again and again, and then I was holding her, wrapping my arms tightly about her shoulders. But she pulled away, stooped, doubled over with weeping, and I felt the immensity of pain within her—heavier than the world that she bore on her back.

Zeus gets what he wants.

The shape of what had happened, above world, while I'd passed my time below it, began to form in my mind like jagged barbs. I gazed at my mother. My mother—what had Zeus done to her? The pain within me gave way to a burning spite, and I sat down, weak, on a green cassock that molded to my body, growing up and around me, vining, flowering.

This bower was the only green thing left in a wintered world.

"Mother," I said, trying to find my voice. "Mother...what happened?"

She wiped her face, shook her head, knelt down before me and brushed her hand over my forehead. "It doesn't matter now. But, Persephone, what happened to you?"

"I left," I told her. "I left you."

Her eyes were bright. "You did a good thing. You did what you had to. I'm glad you did it, Persephone. It saved you, I think. For awhile." She leaned forward, pressed her lips against my ear. Her whisper was softer than breath: "You shouldn't have come back."

She smelled of crushed flowers, broken earth. I stared at her wide-eyed, but she shook her head, pointed upward.

Fear descended upon me, a dark shadow dangling in the cavity of my chest. My mother gathered my hands in hers and bent her head. She shed tears upon my fingers.

~*~

I dreamed I was in a round hole in the earth, walls of dirt towering overheard. I could see a sliver of moonlight above, but the walls were closing in, and dirt rained down upon me, and I couldn't scream, because the earth filled my mouth, and I was buried, buried, lost.

I woke, the sensation of suffocation too real, and I coughed for a long moment into my hand, in the dark. My mother was gone from the bower, melting snow and ice, reseeding the planet—as she had been ordered to do.

By Zeus.

I lay in the dark—the safe, familiar dark—and imagined myself somewhere else. What was Hades doing now? I tried to sleep again, tried to call up dreams of her, but I couldn't relax. I paced the tight confines of the bower, and—skin prickling in the cold air—walked out into the night. All was silent, save for the soft shifting of tree branches as the snow melted and fell. There was a sharp scent in the air, of blood, and I could scarcely see my hand before my face.

"Persephone?"

A dream. I was dreaming. I was still lying in my bed, asleep, and I dreamed that Hades—that Hades was here—

I stiffened, as she spoke my name again.

No. This was real. I was awake.

I turned to her, heart rattling against my bones. And a third time, she said it, my name, syllables dripping like honey from her tongue, and I was running in the dark, slipping over the ice, tripping over the dead, tangled vines and into her arms.

"You're here," I whispered, reaching up, feeling the planes of her face beneath my hands. I didn't know what else to say or do; I pressed my head against her breast, heard the steady heartbeat there.

"Of course I'm here," she laughed easily, holding me at arm's length. It was a sudden movement, and it was too dark to see her clearly, and my breath caught in my throat. I stared at her, transfixed.

Her black eyes, even in the darkness, shone.

"Hades?" I whispered, reaching for her again, tracing my fingertip over her lips. "Am I dreaming?"

"Surely not," she laughed again, a laugh clear as bells, and she bent her head to kiss me.

Her mouth was hungry and hard and pressed roughly against my lips. I broke away, heady, desperate for air, but she drew me close again, held me too tightly, hurt me, and I pushed against her shoulders, pushed her away. She stepped backwards, swiping the back of her hand over her mouth.

"My Persephone, precious Persephone." She offered a conciliatory hand to me as my pulse thundered in my head. "You look lovely, so lovely. And what a pretty necklace that is around your lovely neck."

There was a roar in my ears, all around me, as my mind raced with thoughts of swans and bulls and shapeshifting gods. "Do you like it, Hades?" I whispered, my voice sharp as claws.

"It's very pretty," she said again, reaching for it.

"Don't you dare touch it."

I didn't know what was happening—the earth was moving, crumbling apart, and the roaring had escaped my head, now rushed and wailed all around us, and the trees shook, snow falling in heavy clumps, and I pointed my hand and called the liar by his name.

"Zeus," I whispered, and everything went still.

"Don't be foolish," said Zeus evenly, still wearing the shape of Hades. It was perverse; he held out his arms to me in a gross mimicry of my wife. "Don't you know me?"

"You monster."

"Well—" And Hades' face melted, morphed, and as the skin sloughed away, fell all around him, Zeus began to glow. He dazzled, but I would not shield my eyes. I stared at him with bare loathing; I was so full of it, I tasted its bitterness in my mouth.

We watched one another, Zeus and I, like two animals preparing for a fight. He glowed enough to light the forest around us, but I kept my eyes on him, on his contemptuous face.

"You see, I am king," he said, "and kings do as they please. If you try to stop me, if you will not let me have my way, my dear daughter, then I will have to do…things. So sit still and play nice." And he came for me.

It began as a tiny spiral in my heart, the fear that grew and grew and chased me in circles. "What things?" I asked, trying to summon the confidence that came with rage, but it hid from me, and I stepped backward, cringing.

"It must have been frightening for you, when the dead revolted. Was it, Persephone? Now, how hard do you think it was for me to put those events in motion? How easy do you think it would be for me, now, to wave my hand, to destroy *her*—" he spat the word "—and her entire rotting kingdom? I permit it to exist simply because I need to put the dead somewhere. But I could find another place, another *lord*, and easily."

"She's one of the elder gods, older—and far wiser—than you." I glared at him, though I still trembled. "You couldn't destroy her. You wouldn't dare."

"I have destroyed better than her." He snorted. "A goddess no one thinks of, except with scorn. A goddess no one worships because they *fear* her—little do they know…" he laughed, eyes alight, shining. "Now, to get what I came for…"

He reached for me—he grabbed me with his enormous hands, and he tore my tunic, and he put his mouth on my skin, and the blood pounded and rushed in my ears, a crescendo so white hot and terrible that it poured out of my hands, out of my eyes, out of every inch of my body, a white hot light that turned green at the last possible heartbeat.

Zeus had tortured my first love, and he had stolen me away from Hades, plotted to murder her. He had abused my mother, and how many other mothers? How many people had he hurt? Was there anyone who hadn't been scarred by him, by his selfish whims?

Hades had compared me to the stars, and I felt like one now, burning, burning—so hot, I had to explode.

Zeus held me still, but his mouth was open wide in shock, and when he realized what was happening, what was about to happen, it was already too late. There were newborn vines and briars all around us, flailing and whipping and spiraling about him, dripping with silver poison, wrapping around him, tightening, squeezing, dragging him away from me, far enough away for my leaping heart to calm.

He bellowed in rage, twisted out of the vines' grasp, even as more and more roared through the hole in the earth I had created with my wrath, tightening, lengthening, knotting around him. He tore them off, and they grew again, over and over and over.

I leaned against a tree and watched him struggle.

Finally, mired so deep, encapsulated in the green, heaving mass of feverish life, he cried out: "I yield, I yield!"

I didn't trust him—how could I ever trust him?—but my anger had seeped away, sated. I sliced my hand through the air, and the vines stopped writhing; they grew slack, cut themselves off at the quick, so that Zeus had to disentangle himself.

He struggled and cursed, flung words at me too terrible to remember.

When he stumbled out of the heart of the growth, his body was lacerated, bleeding, silver poison leeched into his skin, making it translucent and blue.

It would take his body long to overcome this poison—the poison of my hatred for him. He had to limp home now, or risk weakening beyond anything he'd experienced ever before, perhaps beyond the point of healing.

"You will suffer," he murmured as he stared at me, eyes flashing, dangerous, a vicious, wounded animal. I raised my arms, aimed them at him, and the great god Zeus flinched and cowered, moving quickly, tripping as he ran away from me, into the darkness. I collapsed on the cold, vine-strewn ground, shaking.

My mother came. I heard her running up behind me, crying out my name, but I closed my eyes, pressed my hands to my face. "Oh, Persephone, what have you done?" she whispered, drawing me to her. "Oh, Persephone, what have you done?"

"What I needed to do," I said wearily, heavily. She hadn't seen; she didn't know what Zeus had intended to do to me. I swallowed and bit my lips—

bruised, the skin broken—as she looked down at me, bewildered, her face pale and exhausted.

Zeus always gets what he wants, she'd told me.

Not this time.

I stared down at the ground, at the vines that began to curl at my feet, flower buds bursting open as I gazed at them. There was a heady feeling that rushed through my body then, as I plucked a flower I had grown, held it out to my mother.

She took it, silent.

"What now?" she asked, as if I knew, as if I had any answers.

"I don't know," I said, truthfully. The flower blossomed again, two-headed, in my mother's open palm.

I felt pain and emptiness and heartache and sadness and a hundred thousand things as we sat close, together, in the starless dark of night.

But I felt no fear.

~*~

My mother's urgent shaking woke me, her hands on my shoulders, fingers gripping my skin tightly.

"Persephone, get up," she muttered, pulling at my arms as I toppled off of the grassy cassock. "You have to get up. You must see this..."

I stumbled after her, out of the bower and into the cold morning. She stood like a sentinel, back straight, not stooped, pointing up at the sky.

And there, above us, Olympus crumbled.

The towers fell apart; the palace shattered.

Only the gods could see Olympus, but it had never looked so close or so fragile. It was falling, and it was breaking, and Olympus was the realm of Zeus, and I knew, in that moment, that it changed as he did, a reflection of him.

I shook, could not stop shaking, as I took my mother and I embraced her. Her eyes were far away, and when she spoke, her voice was regal, soft, calm. "We've been expecting this. He has been slipping in power." She looked at me, really looked at me, holding my shoulders out at arm's length. "We have a meeting place; the gods will be gathering there. We need to discuss what to do now..." There were tears in her eyes, but she did not shed them, and my mother smiled. She was beautiful.

"I have to go." I kissed her cheek, wrestled out of her embrace, grinning like a fool. It was over. Zeus' reign of power was over. Maybe I weakened him enough; maybe the other gods found him afterward... Did it matter? It did not matter to me.

I ran through the forest toward the entrance to the Underworld, and I could not breathe deeply enough; for euphoria pumped through me, and my legs moved swifter than wind, and I floated through the Immortals Forest like a dream, until I was in the center, in the heart, and through the gateway and the door and down the path, like lightning, like light. I could not run fast enough.

I was in the hallway for a year and for a heartbeat—I do not remember if the barge was there, or if I called it up. What mattered was that I was in the Underworld, on the other side of the river Styx, and I paused to catch my breath, to breathe, and my heartbeat thundered against my chest as a very cool, sallow wind brushed my cheek, and I stood up and straight and tall. I was queen here now, too, and I knew its secrets: only ill winds blew in the Underworld.

"Persephone!" Pallas was running toward me, eyes wide. She embraced me quickly, and then she was pulling me toward the far wall. "Persephone, he came for her—he came because of what you did to him."

It was not fear but the daughter of fear that came and ate me up, then. It was anger.

"Zeus," I whispered, and started toward the wall, but Pallas was shaking her head, pulling me back. I plucked at her fingers on my garments, and I ran; we ran together.

I heard them before I saw them, heard the great keening from a thousand throats, from a hundred thousand. The dead cried out, and when I saw it, I stopped, I had to stop. There the dead gathered, and there was Zeus in the center, and there was Hades, standing above the others, and I heard her before I saw her, for the very ground of the Underworld shook from her great and terrible whisper.

She said, "You will not harm what I love ever again."

The dead cried out in one voice, and they began to move. Zeus cried out, too, and it was a scream of fear. I ran toward them, Pallas at my heels, and I did not know what to do until everyone and everything stopped.

"Persephone!" Zeus and Hades called out together, one in fear and one in triumph. Hades leapt off of the outcropping of rock, and in a moment, she was in my arms, but Zeus cried my name again, and my eyes snared his.

"Persephone," he yelled, bellowing as the dead pressed against him, swarming him with their bodies. He reached out his hands to me. "Persephone—tell them I am not all bad."

I opened my mouth to speak, but Hades shook her head, drew me closer. "You are not all bad. No thing is," she said, and again the rock and earth resonated with her words, until they sunk into our very bodies, humming through our bones. "But stories repeat, and your time has ended. It will come again. But not now, Zeus. It's over."

"I cannot stand to be in there!" he screamed, and I knew then what the dead intended, saw the opening to the pit of Tartarus in the wall of the Underworld, saw their progression, saw Zeus' ultimate prison: the cell he'd crafted so cunningly would now be his home.

And the earth came up and seemed to swallow him. One moment, the king of the gods stood on the plains of the Underworld. And then he was gone, the dirt shaping itself once more into the entrance of Tartarus. Gaea had taken him back.

With a single voice, the dead cried out. Hades swept me up and held me close, never to let go again, as the sound rose about us, a crescendo of jubilation.

"Welcome back, my queen," she said, and dark eyes shining, Hades saved me.

After

I'm walking along the sidewalk, ballet flats soggy, rain pelting my hair, my jacket, my jeans. I turn up my collar and touch the rail lightly as I run down the subway steps, tracing with my hand the mosaic on the tunnel wall.

Down here, it smells of piss and unwashed bodies, fast food containers and designer perfume, and the warm rain makes the stench worse, and water pours in little rivers down the stairs to mix with the grime of the walkways, with the dreams and depressions of an entire New York City.

They follow behind me like the tail of a kite, a line of dead streaming through the throngs of the living.

That's the pact, that's what was decided, after the fall of Zeus and the Immortals' War. It was millennia ago, but we still hold by it. Hermes herds the dead six months out of the year, and I gather them, guide them during the other six months. It's my job, my purpose, and if there weren't rules, the world would fall apart. I believe in keeping promises.

Like lost children, they follow me. I coax them along, smiling over my shoulder.

My heart is floating, rising within me as I move through the turnstile, the creak of metal like music.

The queen of all the dead, my beautiful wife,

is waiting for me.

I'm coming home.

It's far down from the edge of the platform to the tracks, and a sign tells me to mind the gap, but this is when the magic begins, and the people milling about don't quite see me, not as I truly am, and the ghosts are right behind me, a billowing tribe of mortals who have found commonalities in their joys and miseries, who are now one, one, one, who will come with me, willingly, to the land of the dead, who will create for themselves there a new sort of a life, an existence steeped in possibility.

I hear him barking before I see him. If anyone on the platform looks, they observe a great, slobbering mass of a dog bounding, desperate, nudging at my hands, but I see his three dear heads, his monstrous eyes rolling with pleasure at sight of his mother. He's come to fetch me, he's so ecstatic, and I pet him and laugh as he leaps ahead, races to the Underworld to herald my arrival, barking out with his three mouths that I'm coming, I'm coming...

I bury my hands in my pockets and move deeper into the subway tunnel that turns, seamlessly, slowly, into the entrance to the Underworld. My jeans transform into a dress as red as pomegranates, and my hair streams behind me, and I laugh out loud, anticipation giving my heart wings, and I can no longer wait—I'm running beside the tracks, running because everything I need, crave, want lies before me, below me, down, down, down.

It is the autumn equinox, the feast of Persephone, and—bound by the oldest law the world knows—I'm keeping my promise. I'm coming home. To her.

FIN

About the Author:

Sarah Diemer is a Persephone girl. She tells stories, makes jewelry and runs around after several animals in a lovely, purple-doored house in the country. She likes to think she is funny. When not up to her elbows in glue and words, she hula hoops and gardens, dresses up like a fairy and recites poetry when she thinks no one is looking. She loves her wife more than anything in the universe. You can find out about her new novels, take a peek at the jewelry she makes out of old fairy tales and generally see several sparkly and interesting things at her site, http://www.oceanid.org, or her blog, http://www.muserising.com

Connect with the author at:
http://twitter.com/sarahdiemer
Facebook search: Sarah Diemer, Indie Author

The following is a sneak peek
from Sarah Diemer's next novel,

Ragged:
A Post Apocalyptic Fairy Tale

Coming, Summer 2011!

*Talula is one of very few who survived the Dis-Ease.
Now that most humans are dead, there are rumors
circulating that the remaining number are being
killed by fairies. But how can fairies exist in a
mundane and destroyed world? When Talula meets
Din—who just happens to be a fairy with a desperate
hope—she learns that magic rises even in the darkest
of places, and to save mankind is to save a real and
dying creature: the earth Herself.*

There's a fairy in the barnyard.

My hands go all sweaty on the reins, slipping along the leather as I dismount and push the pony's shoulder over. Maggie snorts, does a little sideways dance, picking up my fear as I duck into the barn, tugging her after me, mind racing. Did the fairy see me? It looked like a girl. Does she know I'm here?

I wrap the reins around a beam and take up the pitchfork. What the *hell* do I think a pitchfork is going to do against a fairy? I mean, it's iron, yeah; Ruth says iron still burns them, but I don't know if Ruth was in one of her old lady episodes or actually knew what she was talking about when she brought it up. I grip the rough handle of the pitchfork and peer through the dirty barn window, set up high on the cinder blocks, cursing under my breath. It would BE my luck. A fairy in the barnyard.

I'm going to die in the barnyard.

"Oh, god, oh, god," I mutter, rubbing at my eyes with a dirty hand. I'm shaking, and I'm afraid, *yes*, I'm afraid, but I'm also really effing *pissed.* I've heard the stories, but I've never *seen* one, you know? But it was a fairy, had to be, because she had wings, and she kind of shimmered in and out of sight. She was too quick to be human, and she was floating about a foot off the ground. Humans don't do that, not that I'm aware of, unless we've had some really weird and ridiculous evolutionary leap among the hundred of us that remain since the Dis-Ease. Actually, I made up that number. I don't know if there are a hundred humans left or a thousand or a million or none, accept for me and Ruth. All I know is that everyone in town is dead, and no one has come to help us, and the one family that wandered through here ranted and raved about how the fairies were killing the survivors, and we didn't believe them because we thought they were sick. I mean, fairies? That's like saying Peter Pan has it in for us, or that lion from Narnia. They're not *real*. But Ruth believed them, and I didn't, and now there's a fairy in the barnyard, and if the stories are true, she's going to kill me.

I peer out, and I kind of feel my heart stop. Yeah. It's a fairy. She's...she's beautiful; she sparkles in a glam rock sort of way, and she's so pale she's almost translucent. She has long red hair, the pretty, curly, Barbie kind, and there are leaves in it, and she wears things that I think a fairy would probably wear, greens and browns, all tattered. She's standing on the ground now, looking right and left, as if she's confused, and she doesn't exactly *look* dangerous.

I walk out of the barn, and I trip on the last step, sprawling. I guess it's because I'm so nervous. The pitchfork sort of flies out of my grasp, and clangs on the dirt, and I'm on my hands and knees in an instant, lunging for it. I stand, crouching, angling the thing toward where I thought I'd seen the fairy last, but she's not there.

Where is she? I whirl and turn, heart stopped, but I can't see her, she's not there, and that means I'm going to die. The blood pounds through my head, and I hold the pitchfork at the level of my heart, and I wonder what will happen to Ruth when I can't take care of her anymore, since I'll be dead and all. Will she die, too? How soon will it be? I left the can opener out this morning, so maybe she can open some cans for a while before she forgets she's supposed to feed herself.

A blur, out of the corner of my eye. The fairy's behind me.

I turn, but it isn't fast enough. She's darted forward, and somehow, the pitchfork is lying ten feet away, and she grips one of my shoulders, and there's something cold against my stomach. I look down, dazed, and see that a glittering dagger is pressed through my coat, and I can feel the point against my skin. I know I am going to die, or maybe I'm already dying, maybe she's already pierced me through, and I just haven't felt it yet, but I look up at her perfect face, expressionless, beautiful like a doll's, with equally creepy eyes, and the first thought I have, the really true and honest thought, is that she's freakin' gorgeous, and I'm angry that the world has gone the way it did, and I've never gotten to kiss a girl.

From *Ragged: A Post Apocalyptic Fairy Tale*
Coming, Summer 2011

CPSIA information can be obtained at www.ICGtesting.com
Printed in the USA
BVOW04s1224040115

381868BV00014B/332/P